grist

grist
a novel

HEATHER
WALDORF

Red Deer
PRESS

Published by
Red Deer Press
A Fitzhenry & Whiteside Company
1512, 1800–4 Street S.W.
Calgary, Alberta, Canada T2S 2S5
www.reddeerpress.com

Credits
Edited for the Press by Peter Carver
Copyedited by Kirstin Morrell
Cover and text design by Erin Woodward
Cover photograph courtesy iStock
Printed and bound in Canada by Friesens for Red Deer Press

Acknowledgments
Financial support provided by the Canada Council, and the Government of Canada through the Book Publishing Industry Development Program (BPIDP).

 Canada

THE CANADA COUNCIL | LE CONSEIL DES ARTS
FOR THE ARTS | DU CANADA
SINCE 1957 | DEPUIS 1957

National Library of Canada Cataloguing in Publication
Waldorf, Heather, 1966–
       Grist / Heather Waldorf.
ISBN 0-88995-347-3
       I. Title.
PS8645.A458G75 2006   jC813'.6   C2006-901290-3

For Beaulah, who knew this would happen.

With many thanks to:
Peter Carver, great editor, great teacher, great person.

The Thursday night group, who helped me hammer out the dents in Chapter 2.

Bonnie, who ate up the whole manuscript, even when it was just a soggy crust with half-baked filling. Was it the chocolate? Your encouragement kept me at it.

And the gang at Resolution, who continue to be so generous with their table space, ice cream, and good humor.

Chapter One

It was a sticky, last-day-of-school afternoon. The halls of Springdale High were ripe with sweaty bodies, old lunch wrappers, and the anticipation of summer. As cheers drowned out the final bell, I slammed my locker door shut and joined the stampede of seven hundred students towards the nearest exits.

Towards summer.

"Not so fast, Charles."

I did an about-face and flogged myself mentally for not taking the south corridor.

With the crook of a gnarled finger, Hector "Tact Is For Weenies" Pollen, my creative writing teacher, summoned me into his dusty lair and motioned for me to sit. Without missing a beat, he launched into a critique of my final assignment, a ten-page mystery he referred to as my "latest literary atrocity."

"Charles, why have you wasted your vast vocabulary and penchant for quick-witted prose on such drivel?" he asked.

I shrugged, feeling sheepish, goat-like, pig-headed, the whole barnyard.

Mr. Pollen stroked his Santa-beard and flipped through the pages of my story, *The Chocolate Moose Man.* "There are two mysteries here, Charles. What happened to the plot? *And,* where's the character development?"

"Mr. Pollen, why do you call me Charles?" I asked, hoping to buy time to manufacture an excuse worthy of my "drivel."

"Charles is a fine name."

"Someone named Hector *would* think so," I muttered.

Mr. Pollen threw his head back and let out a thunderous guffaw, confirming rumors that his booming belly laugh could be heard—and *felt*—clear through to the family studies room two floors up. Just as quickly he composed himself. "Your story has a snappy title and a quirky premise," he admitted. "A rugged, slightly ominous stranger, bearing a six-inch-tall moose whittled from chocolate, appears at a funeral reception. He presents the moose to a small girl and disappears as quickly as he arrived."

"But?"

"But . . . *so what*, Charles? You ended the story too soon. Make me *care* about this man and child. *What happens next?*" Mr. Pollen stared at my face intensely, expectantly, *hopefully.* He told me once that he'd trained himself to be extra observant, that any chance event or encounter might be "grist" for his next writing project. Most students at Springdale—most teachers, too—wrote him off as a nutcase and kept their distance.

I shrugged again. Mr. Pollen could be distracted, but he wasn't gullible. He even had a sign outside his office: *Check Your Shovel At The Door.*

He sighed. "Charles, you seem to have missed a fundamental point I've been trying to make all year; plot and character development are the most important elements of a good story. I suggest you bury this abominable waste of environmental resources and start over."

Mr. Pollen thrust the assignment back at me. "I realize that classes are over, but my final grades won't be submitted until next Friday. You have a week to redeem yourself. Just slide the revised assignment through my mail slot at home."

"And if I don't?"

"You'll get a C-minus. And *that*, Charles, won't be a mystery; it will be a tragedy."

On a different day, I might have graciously taken back my unworthy "waste of environmental resources" and assured Mr. Pollen half-heartedly that I'd give his suggestions some thought. But that day I was hot, hungry, distracted, and fed up with entertaining delusions of becoming a writer when it was so blatantly obvious that I sucked at writing. Better to accept it and steer myself down another career path. Circus performer maybe. Or Zellers cashier.

Or Drama Queen. Without warning, months of frustration deployed like an airbag. *"That, sir,"* I shouted, gesturing at my pathetic assignment, *"is the best I can do!"*

Mr. Pollen scoffed, "It most certainly is not, Charles."

"Stop calling me Charles!"

Mr. Pollen took off his glasses and set them on the desk. With his left index finger he rubbed the bridge of his nose until a red mark appeared, a sure sign I was giving him a headache. He looked up at me and let out a long breath. "What's wrong? I know things must be difficult with your best friend gone to Australia, and your father going to Toronto, and—"

"Mr. Pollen," I interrupted, "with all due respect, please cut the guidance counselor routine." I hated small-town life. Everyone assumed they knew everything about everyone.

Mr. Pollen blinked hard and paused a second, no doubt deciding how to address my insolence. He took the high road and tried to humor me. Bad move.

"Charlena, are you on drugs?" (See, the old geezer *did* know my name. That's right, folks; I am female. Even with no make-up and one of my father's old baseball shirts on, I had a little too much up front to ever be mistaken for a "Charles.")

"No, I am not on drugs!" But maybe I should be? I considered. Weren't there studies claiming pot-smoking boosted creativity? And hey, even if the studies were wrong, I'd be too stoned to care.

Mr. Pollen massaged his left shoulder. "Drinking problem?"

Hardly. I drank beer at parties, but I didn't get invited to enough parties to call drinking a *habit* let alone a problem.

"Pregnant?"

Ha! "No, Mr. Pollen! I just don't want to be a writer anymore. I have nothing to write about."

Mr. Pollen cracked his bony knuckles, loosened his tie, and wiped his sweaty forehead with a crumpled paper towel he pulled from his pocket. "Write from your imagination," he said. "Or about your life. Gather grist! Thornton Wilder said: 'The stuff of which masterpieces are made drifts about the world waiting to be cloaked in words.'"

If what Mr. Pollen said was true, that plot and character development were the most important elements of a good story, then the story of my life was sadly lacking. No recent tragedies. No romantic entanglements. No scandals. No plot; ergo, no character development. Reading my journal—assuming I'd kept one, which I *hadn't* despite Mr. Pollen's relentless prodding—could turn an insomniac into Rip Van Winkle. My life was one big yawn.

"You want me to find the mystery in my life and write about it?" I asked. "My life is cold oatmeal! There is no mystery in my life!"

Unless I counted the Chocolate Moose Man. "Don't take candy from strangers," Mike, my father, had always warned. But I'd taken the chocolate moose anyway, promising myself I'd never tell. I took it and ate it all, managing by some miracle not to get it all over myself. It was the one sweet moment in an otherwise bitter day in my not-quite-four year old life, the day of my mother's funeral. Almost thirteen years later, I still had no idea who the Chocolate Moose Man had been. Maybe I'd even imagined the tall, long-haired hulk with the dark eyes that sparkled. The red, wind-chapped lips turned up in a grin. The stink of oil and cigarettes on his worn leather jacket. The scary silver skull ring on his right pinky. I'd tried for weeks to weave a story for Mr. Pollen from these small memory snippets, but had obviously F-A-I-L-E-D. Fictionalizing additional details about the Chocolate Moose Man to jack up my story seemed strangely dishonest, and searching for the actual missing pieces of his identity would take more time and moxie than I possessed; I was no Nancy Drew. Besides, weren't some mysteries better left unsolved?

Mr. Pollen ahemed. "What are you telling me, Charles—oops—*Charlena?*"

Why couldn't he just call me Charlie like everyone else did? "I'm telling you, sir," I said, tossing my assignment back on his desk. "I'll take the C-minus."

"Any chance you'll reconsider?" He picked up the story and held it out to me, tried to get me to take it back from him, give it another go.

I took it all right. Took it and ripped it into a million pieces right there before his bewildered eyes. Then, in a cloud of confetti, I flounced out of the office without being dismissed.

With the intention of punctuating my exit with a loud, theatrical slam, I turned back to grab the doorknob.

Mr. Pollen had shot me a lot of looks that school year. Amusement and pride at first, then more recently concern and exasperation. But that afternoon, the look I received was more than I bargained for; it speared me to the bone.

Disappointment.

Chapter Two

I set off for home in the sweltering heat, my backpack bulging with twenty pounds of tattered notebooks and my heart heavy with anger. Damn Mr. Pollen. Around me, kids were jaunty with the expectation of pool parties, paychecks, and summer romance. I had nothing to look forward to but two long months of one hundred percent grist-free boredom.

Okay, there were worse fates than mine. After all, I wasn't being sent to a leper colony. Or to Yellowknife without a sweater. Or to summer school, squashed like a mosquito under the gnarled, critical thumb of Hector The Grouch. But come on; I was sixteen. Didn't I deserve more freedom when it came to planning my summer vacation? It wasn't like I had a history of organizing beach orgies or bank heists. Didn't matter. Mike, my dear old dad, had recently served up three options. "Other" wasn't one of them.

Behind Door Number One were ten long weeks in Toronto touring museums and mega-malls with Mike's girl-friend, "Botox" Barb, while Mike taught an accounting course at Ryerson. It was to be my father's first time teaching. His first time accepting a temp job away from our small town. The first time he planned to shack up with anyone since my mother died. Bringing me along for the ride was a bad idea on so many levels that just thinking about it made my head spin.

The second option involved me working at Rocket River Camp. Mrs. Barkley, my homeroom teacher, was the camp's art director; each spring she offered jobs to all her eleventh graders—minus the pot heads, fist-fighters, and vampire wannabes. But two months of wiping homesick noses, dodging Jell-O balloons, and leading "Kum-Ba-Ya" just wasn't the type of summer employment I was cut out for. Especially after Mrs. Barkley admitted that her staff didn't earn *money*—they earned self-confidence and self-reliance and all those other supposedly desirable "selfs." If the nearest Roots outlet accepted those stellar qualities as legitimate currency, I'd aim to be the best-dressed student in twelfth grade come September, but in the meantime, thanks, Mrs. Barkley, but no thanks.

The third and final possibility was for me to spend the summer with Grandma Josie, my mother's mother, at Lake Ringrose. I'd never been up north before. Until I was seven, Grams and Gramps came down to Springdale for a week each Thanksgiving to visit me. Then Gramps died of a stroke, and Grams came alone. A few years ago, I asked my father why we never went to visit her instead. Mike was quick to explain that he couldn't keep up with his work at a primitive cabin.

"You live in a shack?" I asked Grams, horrified. "With no electricity? An outhouse out back?" Images of *Roughing it in the Bush* flashed through my mind.

My father, who was a workaholic before he met Barb, shook his head and blushed. "No, no. It's just that . . . well, Josie only has one phone line." And Grams was quick to add that she *preferred* coming down to visit Mike and me each

October. That it was her "big yearly bus excursion." That the change of pace was "good for her soul." That it gave her the opportunity to visit my mother's grave site and take in what she called the "splendid fall colors" of Eastern Ontario.

That said, it came as a bit of a surprise to me when at the end of May, Grams called while I was at school and asked Mike if I'd like to spend the summer with her. To see the property that would one day be my inheritance. She had no plans of dying anytime soon, Mike was quick to add when he relayed the message to me at dinner that night. But when it *was* Grams' time to move on—to a retirement home *or* to the next life—she wanted to know: would I like the lake house for myself, or should she arrange to sell the property and give me the cash?

With university looming in a year, it seemed like a no-brainer, but Mike took a swig of his nightly Coors Light and pointed out that it would likely be another ten or more years before Grams—"that tough old bird"—was ready to give up her home.

In another ten or more years, I'd be old, too. Older than my mother was when she died.

Mike wiped a blob of Hamburger Helper off his chin. "I understand if the idea of living in a remote lake community doesn't appeal to you."

Of course he'd understand. Mike's idea of an outdoor adventure was bringing his paperwork out onto the back porch.

"But," he continued, "Lake Ringrose is an all-season recreational community. You could rent out the house. The income from all those weekend warriors might support your writing habit."

"In other words, I won't need a real job?" I sneered, resisting the urge to flick a forkful of noodles at him.

"That's *not* what I said, Char," Mike replied, reaching across the table to ruffle my hair. He always called me "Char." I liked the abbreviated nickname when I was younger; lately it made me feel like I was something left too long on the barbecue.

"Look," he continued, "don't feel pressured to visit your grandmother this summer. If you'd rather join Barb and me in Toronto—or work at camp—you can see her next year. Or whenever you want. *Really*, there's no rush," he added. It was no secret that Mike wanted me in Toronto for the summer. Where he could keep tabs on me. Where Barb and I would have to bond or kill each other trying. "Just think about it and let your Grams know your decision."

Decision? Please; it was Grams' or suicide. I'd never survive crack-of-dawn calisthenics at Rocket River Camp or Mike and Barb's so-sweet-it-could-give-you-diabetes romance in Toronto. I was no bear-wrestling, back-to-nature tree-hugger, no more than I was a street-smart, rave-attending urban princess. Either way, I'd be eaten alive.

Was it normal to know precisely who I wasn't, but not have a clue who I was? Last summer, I might have told you— *bragged* even—that I was an aspiring writer with a dorky but affectionate widowed father and a colossal crush on my best friend Sam. But now I'd lost my father to Barb, my career aspirations to Mr. Pollen, and Sam to Australia. Now I was *hollow*—like a Barbie doll, only stunningly mediocre. Average height. No features on my face—or chest—so big or so small that they could be called deformities. Willful, turd-colored curls that took on fantastic Medusa-like qualities if I didn't keep them cut short. Grams always told me that I was beautiful, that my green eyes were expressive, but well-meaning as she might have been, I suspected my Grams was a liar.

I speared a tomato with my fork. "Why can't I just stay home alone this summer, Mike?" I asked. "Dairy Barn will give me full-time hours—*and* free soft-serve."

"Because I'll worry about you."

If Mike had a wart for every time he'd worried about me those past few months, he'd look like a freak. "You'll worry about me anyway," I said.

"True enough," he replied, stifling a burp. "Maybe we should both stay home this summer." He looked strangely relieved at the possibility. "I'll arrange to teach my course online. Barb will understand; she gets a two-month break from Safeharbor either way."

Oh, puke. Barb was a youth counselor at an after-school drop-in center; like some teachers, she got summers off. If her effect on me was any indication, she really sucked at her job.

I shook my head. "Maybe I need some time alone this summer, Mike," I said, passing the rolls.

Mike sunk his teeth into a bun and pondered my suggestion. He chewed and swallowed. "Maybe what you *need* is a change."

Ha. What he meant was that maybe I needed *to* change. I wiped my chin on a paper napkin. "Okay, then. I'll go to Grandma Josie's."

Mike nodded without enthusiasm. His lips struggled not to frown. A thunderstorm flared briefly in his eyes. I blew it off as separation anxiety; it would be the first time he and I spent a summer apart.

Finishing his beer, my father brought his empty dishes to the sink. "Good dinner, Char."

Jrist

Mike said, "Good dinner, Char" every night, even when the food was under-done, burnt, bland, or just plain horrible; it was part of his dad-like charm. It was also part of our long-standing living arrangement: I cooked and he cleaned.

I didn't ask Mike if he would miss my cooking while I was away at Grandma Josie's. Barb was a great cook. It was the thing I hated most about her.

Chapter Three

I was forty minutes late getting home that hot afternoon. Two paces into the house I was confronted with the familiar *rat-a-tat-tat* of Mike's computer keyboard behind his office door.

I tossed my backpack in a corner and peered into the kitchen and living room. No sign of Barb. Maybe the day was looking up.

When Mike informed me last December that he and Barb—an Ottawa woman he met at a regional bowling tournament a few years back—were "serious," I laughed. Hard. (Never fear; I was soon paid back tenfold for this gross act of insensitivity.)

Mike's face fell.

"You're serious?" I'd scoffed. Stupid me had just figured she and Mike would go on being bowling buddies forever. I never suspected that all those times Mike called to say he'd be home late, that he and Barb were "going for coffee," that it might be a code phrase for . . . well, never mind.

"Serious."

Then, only three days after the Barb bomb dropped, my best friend Sam told me that his family was moving to Canberra at the end of January. At first, I just thought he was referring to a new subdivision out on the highway. But no, he was referring to Australia—about as far away from Springdale as you can get without a rocket.

Wh . . . wha . . . *why?* I sucked in my breath and prayed for the floor to stop spinning. Sam's father worked for the federal government; he'd been given a promotion and a year-long posting Down Under. Sam was given the choice to go, or to stay in Springdale with his Aunt Carol so he wouldn't lose his spot in the techno-gifted program at Springdale High. I let out a *whoosh!* of relief. Sam didn't have to go. He'd stay for sure. Ha. Sam said he'd rather eat a bowl of steaming koala dung than give up a chance to commune with kanga-roos. He even negotiated a deal with the Springdale School Board to finish his eleventh-grade course work on-line. Did Sam ever consider that I might miss him, or that my friend-ship might be worth more than a bushel of kiwis?

"What if a year turns into a permanent posting?" I demanded. I knew how these things worked. Eleven years ago, another Springdale family was transferred to Madrid for six months. They were still there.

Sam shrugged. "It's not like Springdale is the center of the universe."

Was there any point telling him he was the center of mine? The answer was no.

The night before Sam left for Australia, he stopped by after dinner to say goodbye. Mike was on his way out to meet Barb when Sam skidded up our driveway on his old bicycle and leaned it against the side porch the way he'd been doing since he got his first two-wheeler. There wasn't much snow that winter, but Sam was quick to gloat that in January it was summer in Australia.

Rub it in, already.

"How's it going, Sam?" Mike asked, as Sam ducked through the kitchen doorway—he was six-four and growing—and pulled off three bulky wool sweaters. (His grandmother was a knit-a-holic. Sam had more sweaters than anyone I knew. He never wore a coat, just kept layering his sweaters until he was warm.)

Sam gave him the thumbs up, dropped his bicycle helmet on a chair, and ran a hand through his messy red mop of hair.

"Looking forward to the big move?"

"Can't wait," Sam grinned. Damn if he hadn't just had his ugly braces removed; his teeth were radiant.

"How do you think you'll like—"

"Don't you have a *date,* Mike?" I interrupted, nudging him towards the door. Once he and Sam got talking, they could sometimes go on for hours and I wanted what little time I had left with Sam all to myself. "You wouldn't want Cinderella to turn into a pumpkin or however that goes."

Mike pulled on his jacket, saluted me, and wished Sam well with one of those obnoxious, back-pounding guy-hugs complete with loud whoops. Then, grabbing his keys off the counter, he told me not to wait up and *bounded* out the door and down the porch steps to his Caravan. (Nothing like the anticipation of sex to—ewwwww!—put spring into my father's previously unremarkable step.)

Sam and I grabbed Cokes from the fridge and padded down the hall to my bedroom. Just like it was any other day, I stretched out across my futon and Sam settled into the old recliner by the window, propping his size fourteen feet up on my desk.

We drank our pop. Sam burped the alphabet. I scored a point lobbing my empty can into the recycle box by the door on my first try.

Things seemed like usual, except that Sam was leaving in the morning—maybe forever—and my heart was in my throat.

Okay, get over it already, you're saying. But Sam Garrison had been my friend, my *best* friend, my *only* real friend, since we were babies. Years ago, his mother and mine worked together at the Springdale Professional Center. My mother was a nurse; Sam's was the receptionist. Sam and I were born just two weeks apart and we'd spent at least part of every day together since. Over the years, Sam had morphed from a red-haired runt into a towering teenage techno-wizard, destined to make his first million in computer graphics. I'd become a wannabe novelist, who, if Mr. Pollen had anything to say about it, was destined to specialize in rejection slips. The two of us had always shared a lot of laughs. In recent years, I'd been wishing we could share a lot more, a fact to which Sam was totally oblivious. Thick as his intellect was, Sam had the emotional depth of a birdbath.

"Do you think Madame Dumas will miss me?" Sam asked.

"NO!" I hooted just to spite him. Sam had been harboring a mad crush on his French teacher for over two years. He even joined the after-school French Club so he could be near her, despite the fact he hated conjugating French verbs and memorizing "Pierre and Monique" dialogs.

"You realize, Sam," I added, "that Madame Dumas is at least forty years old. You're jail bait."

"She's beautiful," Sam mused.

"Her husband is a plastic surgeon, you idiot!"

Sam threw the chair cushion at my head. "Go ahead and laugh. What would you know about unrequited love?"

"More than you'd think," I let slip.

Sam smirked. "Ha. Who have you ever been in love with?"

I weighed my options. If I refused to tell him, he'd call my bluff. If I chose an arbitrary name from our class at school, it would surely come back to haunt me when I least expected it. If I was honest, my life would change instantaneously for better or worse and I wasn't sure if my reduced-plot lifestyle was ready for the shock.

But Sam was leaving in fourteen hours. It was now or never. I took a deep breath and threw caution to the wind. "I love *YOU*, you jerk!"

This was the part where Sam was supposed to declare he loved me, too. Agree to stay in Springdale forever. Take me in his arms and kiss me until I fainted. Instead—here was my payback for scoffing at Mike and Barb being "serious"—Sam bust a gut laughing. Coke came out his nose. "Hahahaha, Charlie!" he snorted. "I'm going to really miss joking around with you!"

"You know, Sam," I said, glancing at the clock over my desk. "It's getting late and you've got a big day tomorrow. I think maybe we should call it a night."

"What? It's only seven-thirty."

"You should probably get home. Make sure you haven't forgotten to pack your zit cream." I shooed Sam out of my bedroom and towards the porch. On the way, I plucked his bike helmet from the kitchen chair and plunked it up on his head a little more roughly than I'd intended. After he'd pulled on his sweaters and boots, we hugged quickly, *platonically*, and I told him I'd miss "joking around" with him, too. "Have a safe trip!" I waved cheerfully, then slammed the screen door after him. "You big, dumb dog," I muttered.

Slinking back to my room, I crawled into bed without getting undressed. Pulling the covers up over my head, I clenched my eyes tight, chewed my lip, and wondered if a) grist-gathering was always so emotionally hazardous, and b) if heartbreak and humiliation could be fatal.

Now, almost five months later, I was still wondering.

Chapter Four

You might think that if *anyone* could understand my heartache about Sam, it would be Mike; after all, after my mother's death, hadn't it taken him more than a decade to start dating again? Hadn't he spent *years* hiding under a mountain of paperwork behind his home office door? Hadn't I found him more times than I could count holed up in the basement den with the wedding album cradled in his lap? Okay, I knew that Sam's moving to Australia wasn't the same as dying, but if Sam *had* died, at least I'd have known it wasn't his *choice* to leave me.

Now I pounded on my father's office door with my fist. "Hey, Mike!" I shouted.

"Char? Is that you?" he called.

I poked my head through the door. "No, Mike. It's Shania Twain. Superslices or the Colonel?"

Mike swiveled in his chair to face me. "It's Friday already?" he asked, referring to our long-standing Friday night "pizza or chicken" routine.

"Time flies when you're digging tax shelters. What'll it be?"

Mike glanced at his watch. "None for me, thanks. Barb called earlier and asked if I could pop over tonight. She needs help putting together a new IKEA bed."

"Did you wear out her old one?" I asked, though trust me, I *didn't* want to know. It was just that making Mike blush was one of the few pleasures remaining in my life.

"Very funny," Mike said. According to family folklore, I inherited my sarcasm and off-beat sense of humor from my mother. Judging from old family photos, I also inherited her wide hips, but so far everyone had been too polite to mention it, at least in front of me.

"Want to go into Ottawa *with* me tonight?" Mike asked. "The bed won't take long. We could all go out for pizza. Or maybe catch that new Tom Hanks movie? I'm sure Barb's boys would like to join us."

"I'd rather stick pins in my eyeballs." Every time Mike mentioned "Barb's boys" I had to fight off a desperate urge to rip his throat out. Barb's boys were burping/farting/nose-picking fourteen-year-old triplets who worshiped Mike because he was fluent in Canada's third official language: hockey. Huey, Louey and Dewey (they had real names, but I could never remember them) were leaving for Vancouver soon (hip, hip, hooray!) to spend their court-appointed summer vacation with their father. From eavesdropping on Mike's late-night phone conversations, I knew Barb's ex-husband was a first-class slimeball—he'd left her for his nineteen-year-old secretary while the triplets were still breast-feeding. It didn't take a genius to know that Three-Breasted Barb wasn't looking so much for a new and improved husband in Mike as she was a new and improved father figure for her terrible trio. But for sixteen years I'd ridden shotgun in my father's life; I resented being relegated to the now-crowded back seat.

"Everything go okay at school today, Char? You having second thoughts about leaving for Josie's on Sunday? You seem—"

"I'm fine, Mike," I interrupted. "It's just . . . *Fatal Attraction* is on TV tonight. I can't miss that."

Mike sighed and dug into his pocket for his wallet. He offered me a twenty. "Order whatever you like for yourself, Char."

I waved off his money. "I won't bother with take-out. I'll just nuke some soup later."

Mike's eyes were sad. "Can I at least bring you home a doggie bag?"

Arrfff. "Sure, Mike. Maybe a few milk bones and a flea collar, too."

Later that night, I sat alone on the couch, *again,* trying to fill the emptiness gnawing at me with angry movies and junk food. I had nothing to show for all those hours except ten extra pounds on my hips. A better person might have used all that spare time to improve herself, or at least exercise and keep up with her homework. But as my weight climbed, my grade-point average nose-dived.

Mr. Pollen *would* be the one to notice my crash and burn. Mr. Pollen, who pushed and prodded and cajoled. Mr. Pollen, who tore my writing apart like a real editor would— or so he said. Mr. Pollen, whose brutally honesty observations were diamonds in the rough—rough as a scouring brush. Mr. Pollen, who in his inimitably irritating way, *cared.* About my writing at least. Until I blew him off.

I briefly considered calling him to apologize for my tirade that afternoon. But I knew that Mr. Pollen would say that he didn't want an apology; he wanted me to "make him care" about the Chocolate Moose Man. So instead of picking up the phone book, I retreated to my room and kicked back in my old recliner—Sam's recliner! Staring out my bedroom window at the man in the moon, I decided that the best thing I could do for Mr. Pollen, myself, the Chocolate Moose Man, and the literary community at large, was this: NEVER WRITE AGAIN.

Chapter Five

Sunday morning, Mike was at the kitchen table, his head buried in the *Pulse*.

The *Pulse* was Springdale's twice-weekly community newspaper. Leaving the wars, epidemics, celebrity scandals, and stock market news to the major Ottawa papers, the *Pulse* was bursting with birth and death notices, minor hockey bulletins, and local politics. People read it for the gossip and sale announcements, and to clip photos of neighborhood kids posing with their soccer teams. I worked as a summer intern at the *Pulse* last summer, though I could have made more money in less time dredging ditches around town for tin cans. Mr. Pollen recommended me for the job; he assumed I'd find licking envelopes, fetching Timbits, and writing community service announcements challenging. The *Pulse* downsized its staff last fall and wasn't hiring summer students anymore. Just as well. I made terrible coffee, or so Joe, the managing editor, used to tell me every day.

Mike looked up when I walked into the room. "Morning, Char."

"You missed your curfew, Mike." I was joking, but *honestly*, it had been past two a.m. when the Caravan pulled into the garage and woke me. Like it wasn't enough that he was

first

29

out past midnight on Friday? He had to go out again the next night, too?

Mike blushed. "The triplets are flying out to Vancouver this morning. They said to tell you goodbye."

"Uh huh." Goodbye triplets. Good riddance. I could just imagine a bleary-eyed, heavy-hearted Barb loading bags of boy-things into her car trunk. Swigging black coffee from a one-liter travel mug. Offering her "darling sons" hugs and homemade cinnamon buns. Dispensing last-minute advice about how to get along with their "difficult" father in the weeks ahead. Ha. Barb's spawn *loved* spending each summer in British Columbia. If she only knew what her "three precious boys," my God-help-me potential *step-brothers,* told me about the parties and extreme sports and wild girls in Vancouver when her back was turned, Barb might pull out her hair, have a nervous breakdown, or, at the very least, *frown.*

Sighing, I settled into my chair and poured my Cheerios and milk. Mike and I had been eating the same breakfast for the past thirteen years: Cheerios, sliced banana, apple juice. I was leaving for Grams' the next day; I hoped she knew to stock up.

Mike let out a whoop. "Oh no!"

"What?" I asked, setting down my banana.

No reply. I watched Mike's eyes dart back and forth across the page.

"What is it?" I repeated, my chest pounding.

Mike looked at me then, the same look he gave me when I was eleven and he sat me down to break the news that Bart, our eighteen-year-old tabby, had curled up in his favorite chair and died. Just like that. No warning, no pain.

"*What happened, Mike!*" I shouted. "*What's wrong?*"

Mike lay the paper flat on the table and read out loud. "The Springdale Seniors Book Club is canceled until further notice." He paused and looked up. "Hector's had a heart attack."

"Hector? Who's Hec . . . *Mr. Pollen?*"

Mike nodded.

Oh, my God. "Is he . . . ?" I couldn't say it. Years ago, when Gramps had died suddenly, he'd been really old, fifteen years older than Grams, well into his seventies. It was sad, but "not unexpected," Grams said when she called to tell us. But Mr. Pollen? No way.

Mike shook his head. "He's still alive. But his condition sounds grave. The article says he had emergency quadruple by-pass surgery Friday night."

It was a mistake. A typo. "Mike, I was talking to Mr. Pollen Friday afternoon. He was fine." Okay, he was pale and tired-looking, but I thought that was just because of the heat and me being such a pukehead.

Mike pointed a stubby finger at the article. "The heart attack happened around dinnertime. Hector was at the IGA, buying a roast chicken. He keeled over in the checkout line." Leave it to the *Pulse*'s gossip-mongering wanna-be-big-city-reporters to get the entire sordid scoop.

I stared down at my Cheerios. I'd been famished three minutes ago; now I wanted to heave.

"Are you okay, Char?" Mike asked. "I know Mr. Pollen is your favorite teacher."

I slammed my spoon down on the table. "He is *not* my favorite teacher! He's a *jerk!*"

"You don't mean that, Char. Don't talk that way," Mike said.

I didn't want to talk at all. "Pass me the sports page, would you?" I asked.

Instead, Mike folded the paper and put it aside. "Char?"

"Yeah?" I picked up my spoon and shoveled in a huge mouthful of cereal. But my throat had closed. I couldn't swallow. I started to gag. Finally, I managed to spit the Cheerios back into the bowl.

Mike was calm. "Char?"

"I don't want to talk about it."

Mike sat with me for another few minutes while I stared down at my soggy cereal and bit at the inside of my cheek until I tasted blood. Finally he rose from the table. "I'll be in my office this morning," he said. "If you change your mind and want to talk—about *anything*—just let me know. Maybe we can call the hospital later, or see if—"

"Won't Barb be coming over when she's through at the airport?" It wouldn't be Sunday without Barb's goddamn cheerful presence in our house. Her fucking delicious meat loaf in our oven.

"I'll call and tell her not to come."

"Don't bother."

"Char?"

"I'm fine, Mike." I got up and tossed my cereal bowl in the sink. "People have heart attacks all the time."

I spent the better part of the day hiding in my room, avoiding my father's concerned glances, packing for my trip to Lake Ringrose, and, even though I wasn't raised to be the praying sort, praying. I made a million deals with God. If Mr. Pollen got better I'd give up salt and vinegar chips for the rest of my life. I'd take up jogging. I'd floss more often. And oh, God, please don't ever let the same thing happen to Mike. Not until he's at least ninety. Or a hundred.

My father, true to his word, stayed home all day in case I wanted to talk, which I didn't. Mike even called Barb and told her that since it was my last full day at home, it might be nice if he and I spent some time alone. He didn't tell her that I was having a crisis. He even ordered pizza for dinner—Hawaiian, my favorite—but I still wasn't hungry.

Before bed, I joined him on the worn leather couch in the living room. Together we watched an old episode of *Seinfeld*. For Mike's benefit, I laughed at all the appropriate moments, but I wasn't fooling anyone. Mike flipped the TV off when the credits rolled and stretched a burly arm around my shoulder, pulling me towards him, and kissing my hair the way he used to when I was a little kid.

"I know things haven't been easy for you lately," he said.

I stared down at a juice stain on the carpet and willed myself not to blink. Just when I was totally frustrated with the male species, my father had to go and pull something like that. Like *understanding*.

"I miss the way things were," I blurted out. "When it was just you and me—and Sam."

"I know. I do, too, sometimes."

"Yeah, right." I was too old to pout, but I did a good imitation.

Mike frowned. "I *do*, Char. But things change. People move away. People fall in love. People . . . die. The only thing that hasn't changed, will *never* change, is how much I love you." His gaze settled on the big pile of luggage I'd dragged out into the hall. "I still wish you were coming to

Trist

Toronto with me this summer. Barb doesn't feel that the two of you have had much of an opportunity to get to know each other."

"Barb and I have nothing in common."

Mike knew it was true. Like that gift certificate Barb gave me for my birthday a few months ago, for a "spa day" at World Of Women. Give me a break. My so-called morning beauty regimen consisted of brushing my teeth and running a wet hand through my tangles. I thanked Barb for the gift— I wasn't raised in a barn—but I wished secretly that the certificate had been for books or jeans or a few CDs.

"I'll save it for a special occasion," I told her.

"Maybe we could go together one day," Barb had suggested.

"Sure," I'd agreed. After all, one day wasn't *that* day—I'd have time to psyche myself up. Plus, Mike always said not to look a gift horse in the mouth. I tried not to look at Barb's mouth at all. She had one that was always smiling at me. I felt inferior with my sneers and grimaces.

Now I said to Mike, "You're wrong. Barb wants you all to herself this summer. She told me so last week."

Mike shook his head. "Barb *told* you that spending the summer at Lake Ringrose might be a wonderful experience for you. An opportunity for you to learn about more about your mother, your . . . roots."

My decision to go to Lake Ringrose was fueled by escapism, not curiosity. Besides, I already knew about my roots. My mother, Geri, first met Mike at sleep-away camp when she was fourteen. They belonged to rival cabin groups and spent the summer blasting each other with water guns and mashed potatoes. Six years later, they met up again at university. Fell hard for each other. Married at twenty-two.

Had me at twenty-three. Geri died three months short of her twenty-seventh birthday. Mike told me that my mother was funny and artistic and loved singing in the shower. Grams told me that Geri was a good skater, liked peanut butter and banana sandwiches, and was good with animals.

What else did I need to know?

Okay, so maybe I wondered about other stuff sometimes. Like did my mother have flaws and fears and hopes and frustrations? Did she have a dark side? Regrets? Did she struggle with her weight? Worry about waking up with a zit the size of Manitoba? Get her heart stomped on? Give a teacher a coronary? All right, I admit it; the details of my mother's life were sketchy to me. But so were the details of Mike's life, and he was sitting right there next to me.

I gulped. "Mike, if you like teaching, are you going to move us to Toronto?"

"No way! This university gig is a one shot deal; the regular instructor will be back from his sabbatical in time for the fall session. Besides, who'd want to live year-round in Toronto?"

Duh. "Barb?"

Mike shook his head. "She loves her job at Safeharbor. Besides, the boys already have their hockey teams set for next winter."

"Are you going to ask Barb to marry you?" I blurted.

Mike grinned. "We'll see how it goes this summer, but I think yes."

Something heavy fell from my chest into the pit of my stomach.

Mike raised a brow. "You okay with that?"

"If I said no, would you change your mind?"

He paused, but not for more than a second. "Nope."

I excused myself to go to bed.

"Char?" He called after me. "Are you absolutely *sure* you want to go to your Grams' tomorrow?"

"Absolutely," I replied. Ha!

"And you're okay about Mr. Pollen's heart attack?"

Definitely not. "Yeah, Mike. It's not like he's Gramps or anything. He's not family."

"It's a small town, Char. We're all family."

Chapter Six

At the crack of dawn, Mike drove me to the tiny Springdale bus depot to meet a connection to the Ottawa terminal. Once there, I'd transfer to the northbound coach. If all went according to schedule, I'd meet Grams at Wawa by nightfall. Lake Ringrose was another hour by car.

Fourteen hours on the road. My legs cramped up just thinking about it.

"I'm going to miss you, Char," Mike said when the Springdale bus began to board. He slipped me some extra spending money and engulfed me in an awkward bear hug.

I pulled back. "Then come with me, Mike. Tell Barb you had a sudden change of plans. We'll skip Lake Ringrose, stay on the bus, keep going clear to Saskatoon. Just you and me." I mustered a grin.

Mike laughed. "Nice try, kid—and tempting—but I'm getting paid a tidy sum to teach in Toronto this summer, enough to pay your first-year university tuition."

"What if I don't want to go to university?"

"Then you can use the money to start a rock band or open a dog grooming salon or . . . don't be crazy, of course you're going to university. Oh," he added, digging into his jacket pocket, "I've got something for you. Kind of a going-away

grist

37

gift. Barb spotted it at the mall last week and thought you might like it for your stories."

It was a blank book, a spiral-bound journal. Affixed to the glossy pink cover was a google-eyed puppy made of blue fake fur. Attached to the book's spine was a pen-on-a-rope shaped like a bone.

God, Barb. Next time just get me a pack of razor blades.

"Tell her thanks, Mike," I choked.

The bus driver honked. I had to go.

"I love you, Charlie-bear."

"Love you, too, Daddy-Mike."

I took a seat and watched for Mike out the bus window. He waved and smiled at me, his eyes squinty in the early-morning sun. But there was something about his posture, the set of his jaw, the sweat stains under the arms of his T-shirt despite the chill in the morning air. He was probably debating whether it was too late to yank me off the bus and drag me off to Toronto with him and Barb after all.

I did what I could to set his mind at ease. I smiled and waved back.

The coach creaked through downtown Springdale on its way to the highway. I stared out at the rising sun reflected on the windows of the familiar homes, schools, and shops on Main Street. It was like watching my life pass before my eyes.

When the bus turned onto the highway and gained speed, I closed my eyes and laid my head against the window. *Away I go,* I thought, as an unexpected wave of . . . relief? . . . washed over me.

Moments later, I bolted straight up in my seat as another wave, a wave of . . . anticipation? . . . caught me unawares. *Lake Ringrose, here I come.*

I swiveled my head around frantically, trying to catch one last peek of the only life I'd ever known.

But it was gone.

Chapter Seven

I stepped off the coach in Wawa yawning, my butt prickling with pins and needles and my head stuffed with cotton. I took several gulps of cool, damp air, did a few shoulder rolls, and got my bearings.

Not much grist in Wawa, either, by the looks of it—except for that giant iron Canada goose the bus had passed at the Trans Canada turn-off. "'Wawa' is Ojibway for 'wild goose,'" Grams told me years ago when I'd laughed at the funny name. "The area has always been a popular rest stop for Canada geese during migration," she added.

But I didn't see any geese now. All I could make out under the streetlights of the main drag was a grocery store, a few motels, a boat dealership, a liquor store, an Esso station, a—

"Charlena?"

I whirled around. Grams was barely five feet tall but had the well-muscled arms and legs of a woman who has spent her entire life outdoors. Her face was tan and wrinkled—she looked older than her sixty-two years—but her eyes sparkled despite the late hour. She hugged me fiercely and told me how wonderful it was to see me again, that I looked more like my mother each time she saw me.

"How's your father?" Grams asked when she finally let go.

"Excited about teaching in Toronto this summer." I left out the part about Barb tagging along in case Gram didn't approve. I sure didn't.

But Grams grinned. "Isn't it *wonderful* that his girlfriend could go with him to the city? Think Mike will pop the big one soon?"

I shrugged.

"You and Barb get along okay?" Grams asked.

I shrugged again. Barb was just so different from the type of woman I pictured my father falling for. I could imagine— if I *had* to—Mike with a short, wide-hipped, feisty type. Another Geri. But *Barb?* She was taller than Mike by three inches. She had shampoo-ad hair, perfectly tweezed eyebrows, and a flat stomach—how do you *do* that after triplets? She sang along to TV jingles and was always spouting inspirational clichés, like, "If life gives you lemons, make lemonade." I hated lemonade.

"Barb's nice, I guess," I replied, finally. And it was true. But nice in all the wrong ways. Like giving me that spa certificate. Or her trying to get me chatting about hair products. I *got* that she had three boys and was starved for girl-talk, but I *sucked* at girl-talk. I was raised by a man. I'd had a male best friend. I'd *certainly* never aspired to be nominated for Miss Springdale. But now, with Sam gone and Mike in love with a woman who took the girly shit seriously, being one of the boys was also losing its appeal. Just who was I anyway? Certainly no one had called up to profile me on the Biography Channel.

Grams steered me to her car, a muddy, rusted-out, prehistoric station wagon. As I heaved my hockey bag onto the back seat, she asked, "Do you drive?"

"I got my learner's permit last month," I replied. "But Mike hasn't had much time to take me out to practice. My test isn't until October."

Grams tossed me her keys. "No better time to practice than the present. My night vision isn't what it used to be. Never know when I'll hit a moose."

"I don't know," I stammered. I doubted Grams' tin can on wheels had airbags.

"You'll do fine," Grams said, and settled herself into the passenger seat before I had a chance to flat out refuse. "Believe it or not, your mother learned to drive on this same old wagon."

"That's reassuring," I mumbled, then plunked down in the driver's seat and adjusted the seat and mirrors. Grams shooed out the moths swarming the overhead light. When I found the courage to turn the key in the ignition, Anne Murray came blasting out of the speakers at a volume that would have sent me clean out of my seat if not for the seat belt.

"Sorry," Grams giggled, turning the sound down about one notch. "I like a little music when I drive."

We chugged through Wawa without incident; it was almost midnight and the main street was deserted. Shortly after a right turn that took us east past town, Grams motioned for me to hang another right. "Now, just keep going until I say stop," she directed.

The road to Lake Ringrose was a black wilderness, like no road I'd ever traveled before. No houses, no street lamps, no moon even. Just thick evergreen forest on each side of the two-lane gravel road and a hand-painted sign at the turnoff. *Lake Ringrose—30 kilometers.* Grams showed me how to flip on the high beams, which made things about one percent better. I prayed no cars would come charging at us from the other direction. I willed the moose and whatever else lurked in the wild frontier to keep their distance. I hoped that the geriatric vehicle could withstand the bathtub-sized potholes.

Grams kept up a steady stream of questions over the rattle of the engine and Anne Murray's Greatest Hits. I secretly wished she'd fall asleep—or just shut up—so I could concentrate on my driving.

"Do you paint?" she asked.

"Pictures? I'm not much of an artist."

"Geri was a wonderful artist."

I nodded. I had a series of paintings my mother did not long before she died. Mike said I was an early talker and would sit on her bed telling long-winded stories about my stuffed animals. Geri painted vibrant watercolors to illustrate my tales of *Mouse And Hippo At The Beach, Frog and Rabbit At The Mall, Seal and Giraffe Rob A Bank,* etc. and bound them together into a "book." I looked at it every year on what would be Geri's birthday just to let her know I hadn't forgotten the short time we spent together, though to be honest, I had.

"I meant *walls*," Grams clarified. "You're not afraid of heights, are you?" It seemed more of a dare than a question.

I shook my head.

"Wonderful! It's been years since the old house has had a coat of paint. The indoors could use a change, too. Maybe something bright and—how do you kids say it—*cool?*"

"Whatever you like." Home decorating had never been high on Mike's agenda. That might change if Barb and her three stooges moved in with us—I'd live under a bridge before I'd live in *her* house—but for now, things were old and comfortable and *beige.*

"What colors do you like?" Grams asked.

"Anything."

"How do you aspire to be a writer when you seemingly have so little to say?"

"Who said I wanted to be a writer?"

"You did, the last time I visited Springdale. And your father seems to think so, too."

"Mike doesn't know everything about me."

"He says you're a wonderful writer."

"Mike is a numbers man. He wouldn't know a simile from a dangling participle."

Grams frowned. "Are the two of you having troubles? Your father loves you, Charlena. Mike's a good man."

I braced for the next bend in the road.

Forty-five minutes and three thousand potholes later, I turned right and guided the station wagon along an overgrown lane. Tree branches scraped against the windows on both sides like huge animated skeletons. A porch light appeared, seemingly out of nowhere, and Grams pointed out a clearing where I should park. I killed the ignition and let out the nervous breath I'd been holding since Wawa.

"You're a superb driver!" Grams proclaimed and patted me on the shoulder.

Liar, liar, pants on fire, I thought.

As I stepped out of the car, I was almost bowled over. It wasn't Grams' house—a small weather-beaten bungalow with a screened porch running the length of the side facing the lake—that shocked me. It was the smell. One sniff of the heady pine mulch/wood smoke/lake brine/wildflower scent gave me an unexpected jolt of . . . euphoria? And then there was the silence, broken only by the soft pulse of waves against the dark shoreline and the rustle of leaves in the breeze. It was almost musical, like one of Barb's new-age CDs, only for real.

The spell was broken when an army of bloodthirsty black flies declared war on my exposed parts.

Grams dragged my hockey bag from the back seat and passed it to me with a small grunt. "Welcome to Lake Ringrose."

Chapter Eight

Grams made up my mother's old bed for me, but that first night I fell into a dead sleep on the living room couch not five minutes after devouring a snack of hot chocolate and homemade raisin cookies.

Hours later, I woke to morning light, raucous birdsong, and a determined *scratch, scratch, scratch* at the kitchen window screen.

"What the . . . ?" I untangled myself from the thick HBC blanket Grams must have pulled over me and trudged in bare feet over the icy hardwood floor to see what she was up to.

"AAAAAAAAAAAH!" I screamed. It wasn't Grams. There was a wild creature in the kitchen! It had ripped a hole clear through the window screen and was perched in the sink shaking like *I* was the wild creature.

Down the hall a door burst open. Grams scurried into the kitchen and broke into hysterical laughter. She laid a strong hand on my shoulder. "No need for theatrics, Charlena. That's just Gerta. Every few weeks she comes to the window to see what I've got in the pantry. Mind you, she's never barged right in before."

"Gerta?" I was dumbfounded.

"You've seen a little old raccoon before, haven't you?"

"Not up close." And "little old Gerta" didn't seem so little to me. She filled the sink.

"Better get used to the wildlife, Charlena. Plenty of deer in these parts. Sometimes they come and graze right on the back lawn."

"They don't *barge* into the kitchen, do they?" I asked.

The rational presence of my grandmother had calmed Gerta and she began preening like a cat—only bigger. Grams shook her head. "Just the chipmunks sometimes. The odd garter snake. And now Gerta."

"Are there bears?" Maybe it wasn't too late to get Grams to drive me back to Wawa. I could catch the first Greyhound back to Springdale, to civilization.

Grams laughed. "Ah, I've seen the odd black bear, but most of them stick to the woods further north. Any self-respecting bear knows that if it comes around these parts, some crackshot trophy poacher is going to blow its brains to smithereens. I'll show you later how we lock up the garbage to discourage unwelcome visitors."

"What about . . . ?" I pointed to the raccoon in the sink waiting boldly for her handout. "Is she staying for breakfast?"

"Not today." Grams clapped her hands at Gerta, who disappeared back out the hole in the screen, chattering with disappointment. Grams pulled closed the glass pane over the broken screen and locked it. "I'll take out a stale muffin after lunch and leave it up in the tree. I don't want Gerta getting the idea she can claw her way in here anytime. My poor heart can't take you screeching like that first thing every morning."

"Sorry," I mumbled.

Grams shook her head. "My fault. I opened the window last night to air the place out a little. I forgot to close it before bed. My mind isn't the steel trap it used to be," she cackled. "There's a roll of new screening in the shed; we can patch the window up later."

Well, Grams could be sure that *I'd* close the kitchen window—every window in the house—before I went to sleep from now on. What if I woke up one morning with some furry wild creature snuggled into bed with me? I might have been a tomboy by Springdale standards, but put me in the real wilderness and I was suddenly a hysterical female. Mike and Sam would have bust a gut laughing.

After breakfast—yogurt and sliced strawberries sprinkled with a lumpy oatmeal/birdseed blend called muesli—Grams announced that we were going to the village to buy paint. I'd felt a minor stab of homesickness when I realized there'd be no Cheerios that morning. It wasn't like I *loved* Cheerios, but I was used to them; they were the taste of home. So get over it, already, I told myself.

Grams had filled me in on the basic geography of Lake Ringrose the previous night, so I knew that the actual village was another five kilometers along the bumpy road. And that wide trails ran perpendicular to the road on the wooded side that led to seasonal hunting grounds, aboriginal settlements, fishing ponds, and back lots owned by some of the year-round villagers.

"The village store opens this early?" I asked, peeking at my watch. It was barely seven-thirty.

"Not until nine."

"We've got some time, then." Time to go back to sleep for an hour or so.

"Just enough, I'd say." Grams cackled. "You didn't think we were going to *drive* to the village, did you?"

"We're going to *walk?*" I asked. "What about coming home with all the paint cans? I have puny biceps."

Grams chuckled and beckoned me outside into the crisp air. She took an invigorating breath, pulled the door closed behind us, and led me down a steep set of slate steps to a narrow dock. "It's a beautiful morning for a paddle."

I'd never been canoeing before. I wasn't opposed to learning, but what I had in mind for my first time out was a little paddle around the bay, not a ninety-minute voyage.

She tossed me a yellow life jacket and paddle. "You can swim?"

Sure I could swim, but I'd never been swimming in a *lake*. There weren't any lakes near Springdale and no one even *waded* in Springdale's grossly-polluted creek unless they were stupid or drunk. What if a fifty-pound Lake Ringrose fish bit me? Or I became tangled in weeds? Did lake monsters really exist? Why didn't my imagination work like this when I sat down to write for Mr. Pollen? My stomach lurched. Poor Mr. Pollen. He'd probably be at home doing crosswords or watering his marigolds right now if only I'd agreed to rework *The Chocolate Moose Man*.

I looked out across the lake, past the uninhabited islands where Grams said villagers went to picnic, and wondered what this south-shore settlement of fifty-some year-round houses had looked like in the 1920s when the north shore was a gold mine. Over the years, Grams had told me many stories about the hardships faced by the first permanent residents of Lake Ringrose—like my own great-grandparents—who had arrived in the area by Algoma Central Railway to try their hand at mining. It was only after the permanent closure of the mine—and the expansion of the Trans-Canada highway

Trist

49

in 1960—that the recreational potential of the Lake Ringrose area had been developed.

I stood there a few more moments, transfixed, as the sun cast brilliant gold ripples across the water. Three loons puttered around near the shoreline, punctuating the still morning with resonant calls.

Grams laughed at me. "Mother Nature got your tongue?"

It dawned on me (no pun intended) that my mother rose to sights like this every morning of her childhood. She'd grown up knowing natural beauty I'd never imagined until that moment. I wondered if Geri took it for granted, or if she felt dismay years later waking up in our boring old Springdale subdivision. To think I got homesick over something as stupid as Cheerios.

Like her car, Grams' fiberglass canoe had seen better days. Better decades. The once-red paint was faded to a dull pink, and the hull was mostly patchwork from repeated encounters with the rocky shoreline. I took my bow position carefully, supporting my weight evenly across the gunwales like Grams instructed. Even so, it was a challenge not to capsize us or impale myself on the splinters sticking up like daggers from the seat.

In the stern, Grams gripped her paddle with gnarled but competent hands. "Once we finish painting the house, we can spruce up the old canoe here. She's not a beauty, Charlena, but she's seaworthy."

After just ten minutes of struggling with what Grams called a "basic" stroke, my arms and shoulders were numb. It didn't help that the lake breeze became a full-fledged headwind when we rounded the first bend. Grams kept up a steady stream of encouragement. "Keep pulling! You're doing great!

You'll be in tip-top shape by the end of the summer!" I didn't doubt it for a second. I wondered if it might have been less work to sign up for Outward Bound or the Army Reserves.

At five minutes to nine, we pulled alongside the village wharf. I hoisted myself out of the canoe on rubbery arms. My knees ached, my shoulders were paralyzed, and I had what felt like permanent seat ridges in my butt. Grams hopped out of the stern seemingly undamaged, did a few tricep stretches, and tied the boat to the dock with a rope she called the painter.

Grams led me up the wharf and through the village, pointing out a clump of tiny rental cottages peeking out of the trees beyond the beach. The gravel main street sported shops—mostly practical backwoods stuff like sporting goods, hardware, groceries, and video rentals. The post office and liquor store shared a storefront. A workshop Grams said was run by local Cree and Ojibway craftspeople displayed brightly-beaded leather goods and woven blankets in its windows.

"Want to stop for a snack before hitting the general store?" she asked.

My stomach rumbled affirmatively. That bowl of yogurt, strawberries, and birdseed was just a distant memory.

"Jenny's Kitchen" was a small café tucked between the Canada Post/LCBO and a Sears order office.

Grams nodded to a grizzled old man in overalls perched on a stool at the counter. "Hey, Will."

Will's face lit up like a Christmas tree. "You must be Charlena!" He grasped my hand and pumped my arm up and down with enough enthusiasm to power a stubborn well. "This is *such* a pleasure! You're the spitting image of Geri! How long will you be staying?"

"For the summer." If the canoeing and the wildlife didn't get me first.

A tall, angular woman, with wisps of dark hair flying out from under a hair net, bustled out from the kitchen. She wiped her hands on a paper towel. "Morning, Josie. Coffee?"

Grams shook her head. "Two, Jenny. With milk and sugar, please. And a couple of those strawberry scones." She pointed to the display case by the cash register.

Jenny tuned towards the coffee pot, then did a quick double take. She zoned in on me. Her face grew pale and her eyes bulged like she'd seen a ghost.

Grams let out a nervous laugh. "Charlena, this is Jenny. She and your mother grew up together."

"Hi," I said warily. It was weird, meeting all these strangers who'd known my mother better than I ever had the chance to.

Jenny picked her jaw up off the floor. "Hello," she replied with all the warmth of an arctic breeze. She shot Grams a look of . . . confusion? Hurt? Anger? "I had no idea that your granddaughter was visiting this summer."

Grams smiled at me reassuringly. "Charlena, would you run back to the wharf and check that I tied the canoe securely? I'll meet you out front with our snacks in a few minutes."

I wasn't born yesterday; Grams wanted to talk to Jenny in private. Who the hell did Jenny think she was, the town social director? Since when did the proprietor of a backwoods café have the authority to approve all visitors in advance?

I padded down to the wharf and checked the canoe like a good Girl Guide. The rope knot was perfect, as far as I could tell, since I'd never actually been a Girl Guide. I'd eaten a lot of Girl Guide cookies that spring, if that counted.

Frustrated, I kicked some pebbles off the wharf into the lake and wondered—not for the first time that morning—what I'd gotten myself into. Maybe touring the CN Tower and shopping for hair accessories with Barb wouldn't be so bad after all. "Ha!" I laughed out loud.

"Hey, you," said a male voice, startling me.

I wheeled around. It was a guy, maybe a year or two older than me, wearing muddy sweat pants and a life vest, stooping to tie a dented aluminum outboard to the other side of the wharf. Lost in my funk, I hadn't even heard his boat pull in. The guy had a dark brown buzz cut, wrap-around sunglasses, and Brad Pitt lips that—wait a minute; what was I doing staring at his *lips?*

"Hey, yourself."

"You're new?"

"I'm Charlie. Charlena."

The guy straightened up slowly to his full height. He was probably six feet, but all guys seemed short compared to Sam. "I'm Kerry. Kerwin."

"Kermit? Like the *frog?*"

"Just what Lake Ringrose needs—another smartass. It's Ker-*win*. It was my great-uncle's name."

Sounded to me like the sort of tag that belonged on a fat city banker, but oh well; at least he wasn't named Hector.

Hector. Shit. Mr. Pollen told me once that the brain unconsciously seeks out patterns. The something-or-other effect. For example, if we're attracted to someone who drives a blue truck, we'll see blue trucks everywhere. If we want to avoid someone, he or she will turn up around every corner. If we're worried about, say, a sick ex-creative writing teacher, his name will be on everyone's lips. (Did I mention Kerry's lips?)

"Are you visiting someone?" Kerry asked, swatting at a mosquito on his neck.

I nodded. "My grandmother lives at the other side of the bay."

"Your grandmother?"

"Josie Parsons. She's in the café talking to Jenny." I pointed.

Kerry glanced towards the café and frowned. "Jenny's my mother."

I gave his face another quick once-over. "You've got her chin and nose," I said stupidly. The lips must have been a gift from his father's gene pool. "You live here in the village?" I asked.

"Nah. I live over in the A-frame you passed on your paddle into town. The *purple* A-frame?"

Oh. That one.

"Mom's doing. Revenge. She nagged Dad and me to paint the house last summer, but every weekend we'd find an excuse to take off fishing. So she called contractors. They got the whole thing done in the time it took the old man and I to catch a pail of lake trout. My sister, Lisa, calls it the 'Blueberry Puke House'."

"How old is Lisa?" Besides Kerry, I hadn't seen any other young people around. For all I knew, teenagers were an endangered species in this neck of the woods.

"Nineteen. Older than me by a year. She's been at university in Sudbury since last September. Math major. Wants to be a—I can't even pronounce it—*statistician.* She'll come up for a few days at the end of the summer—*if* she can stomach it. Lisa's a *city-girl* now. Like that's something to be proud of. You aren't from a city, are you? No offense."

"Nope. Springdale. Two thousand humans, six hundred dogs, three stoplights, two Tim Hortons—"

"And a partridge in a pear tree?"

"Not even at Christmas," I laughed. "But Springdale—*no offense*—is a booming metropolis next to this place."

"Lake Ringrose will grow on you. Or not," Kerry said, shrugging off the life vest and tossing it into his boat. He extracted a tube of sunscreen from his pocket. He squirted some onto his arms and rubbed it in. "Want some?" he asked me. "Your face is pink. It's easy to get burnt out on the water, even early in the day."

"Thanks." I said, dabbing pineapple-coconut scented lotion on my nose even though I was pretty sure that the "pink" was a biochemical reaction to Kerry, not to the sun.

"KERRY!" Jenny bellowed from the café door. *"KERRY!"*

"The call of the wild," Kerry sighed.

Grams rushed towards me with a coffee in each hand and a paper bag clenched between her teeth.

"Guess I'll see you around," Kerry said. "Hey, Josie!" He grinned at Grams as she approached, then with a little wave in my direction, he started towards the café on legs as slow and bent as an old man's.

Grams handed me a coffee and the bag of scones. "I see you've met Kerry," she said.

"He seems . . . nice."

Grams nodded. "Kerry's a good kid at heart, but . . . well . . . it's not easy being a teenager in this community."

Newsflash, Grams: it's not easy being a teenager anywhere. *"Are there* any other teenagers in this community?" I asked.

Grams tittered. "Worried that you'll only have your old batty grandmother for company?"

"I never—"

"Charlena, I'm kidding," Grams laughed. "I'd guess there are about thirty teenagers who call Lake Ringrose home at any given time. But once the community school lets out for the summer, most go to camp like your mother did, or get jobs at one of the provincial parks along the Trans-Canada."

"What about Kerry?"

"Kerry does odd jobs around the village every summer—carpentry work, boat repairs, landscaping—though," Grams added, frowning, "I don't know how much he'll be able to handle this summer. He recently had an . . . accident." She took a long swallow of coffee and stared out over the lake, the lake that might one day become my summer home.

Or not.

After much deliberation—and ruling out purple!—Grams and I chose banana yellow paint for the house's exterior.

I couldn't believe the general store's huge inventory of paints, brushes, rollers, and all sorts of other indoor and outdoor hardware. I asked Grams who bought it all; I mean, how many light bulbs, paint trays, and fishing rods did Lake Ringrose's tiny population need?

Loading our purchases into the canoe, Grams explained. "It's true that only a handful of rugged souls like myself live here year round. But the summer cottagers start arriving next week; they always need repair supplies, rubber rafts, coolers, lawn chairs. When autumn rolls around, we get hunters who need bullets and windbreakers. Winter brings the cross-country ski enthusiasts and ice fishermen. And—"

I got the picture. "Hard to picture this peaceful place as a tourist trap."

Grams grimaced. "Lake Ringrose will *never* be Niagara Falls, thank God. Nowadays, it's basically just a supply post and trailhead. The village hasn't been booming since the last gold rush, but there's still enough traffic through here year-round to keep the shops afloat."

I wondered what kind of accident Kerry had, what had happened to his legs. "What if someone needs a doctor?"

"We have a doctor. Will Davies is a doctor, *the* doctor. He pulls teeth, too, and does his fair share of veterinary work. Anyone needing a specialist or major surgery gets sent down to Sault Ste. Marie. Emergencies are airlifted out in Will's own bush plane. It's not ideal, but the privilege of living in the wilderness comes with a few concessions."

I pointed back towards the café where I could see Kerry sweeping the steps. He was wearing headphones and doing stiff, awkward dance moves with the broom, clearly oblivious to the fact that he was being watched. Every few seconds, he'd glance over his shoulder at the café door, as if he expected Jenny to come out and yell at him for jerking around. It didn't take a formal inquiry to establish that their mother-son relationship was not the stuff of Hallmark cards. "Grams, why did Jenny react so strangely when she saw me? Why your 'check the ropes' routine?"

"I knew you wouldn't fall for that," Grams sighed. "I apologize for dismissing you, Charlena. It's just that Jenny's one of those people who gets upset by surprises. You look so much like Geri did when she and Jenny knew each other. I should have mentioned to her that you were coming, but I wasn't sure myself until just recently." Grams hesitated a few seconds. "And Charlena?"

"Yeah?"

"I hope you and Kerry become friends, but . . . don't get *too* close. Call me over-protective, but . . . you know what I mean?"

Indeed I did. "Grams, FYI, since you came to Springdale last October, I've had my heart ripped out and forced through a juicer. I'm not looking to have that happen again. Ever."

Grams chuckled, "What young man would *attempt,* let alone succeed, at ripping your heart out? Want me to hunt him down? Stab him with my number seven knitting needle?"

"No. And it was Sam."

Grams raised a brow. "I met him years ago. Wasn't he the little guy with the mess of red curls?"

"Sam is six-four now. He moved to Australia last semester."

Grams reminisced. "Mike used to say that you and Sam were inseparable."

"Apparently not."

"You keep in touch, surely?"

Sure, *Sam* kept in touch. He sent me cheery e-mails and postcards proclaiming "G'day mate!" and "Wow, guess what I did today!" At first, I sent him back equally bubbly e-mails—*lies, lies, lies*—mostly about school. Then, a month ago, Sam had written about an "Elizabeth," a college freshman he met at an electronics shop. "Elizabeth" invited him to go to a computer exhibition with her. Without his saying it, I just knew that "Elizabeth" was taller, thinner, smarter, and funnier than me. Poor Madame Dumas, I thought; Sam had moved on. I hadn't replied to that e-mail. Or the one after. I hadn't even bothered to bring my laptop to Lake Ringrose with me. What would I say to Sam anyway? That I was happy for him and

"Elizabeth"? That I'd actually *volunteered* to spend my summer at Lake Ringrose, where people name raccoons and paint their houses purple? That my insolence and poor writing skills might have killed Mr. Pollen?

"Don't worry, Grams," I assured her. "Kerry is safe from me."

And lake monsters fly.

Chapter Nine

A few days later, Grams served "potluck soup" for lunch. I stared warily at the steaming bowl of lumpy brown liquid, afraid to lift my spoon.

Grams laughed. "I know it looks like diarrhea, but close your eyes and taste it. You'll be hooked."

It was, in fact, *delicious.*

I was washing the dishes and Grams was making her afternoon tea when we heard loud raps at the back screen door. "Avon calling!" a deep voice yelled.

"Sounds more like the Big Bad Wolf," I muttered.

"Come on in, Kerry!" Grams shouted.

Kerry lumbered into the kitchen. "Hey, you," he said to me and began putting away the clean dishes; he knew better than me where everything went. The job finished, he turned to Grams. "I'm taking the boat down to the Marrotts' with a Sears delivery. Maybe Charlie-girl here wants a tour of the shoreline?" Kerry turned to me. He wasn't wearing his sunglasses now and his dark eyes were liquid and inviting, like Hershey's syrup. Get a grip, I told myself. "How about it?" he asked.

Grams looked from me to Kerry, then back to me, like she was deciding a murder case. Were all grandparents this over-protective? Back in Springdale it wouldn't have occurred to me to ask Mike's permission to go somewhere with a guy in the middle of the day. Misguided as it might have been, I wasn't raised to believe that teenage guys were all predators. Besides, I'd taken the karate elective in gym last semester. If there were similar kick-ass strategies to fend off broken hearts, I'd be set for life.

"Oh, go ahead," Grams said after a lengthy pause. "You've done enough painting for one day, Charlena. Dinner's at six. Vegetarian chili and corn muffins. You're welcome to stay, Kerry."

He turned to me. "Don't tell my mother I said this, but Josie's cooking is the best at Lake Ringrose. By far. When I was in rehab, she sent me care packages every week. Oatmeal cookies, cinnamon buns, blueberry turnovers, you name it. Absolutely scrumptious. Mouth-watering. Deeeeee-licious!" He shrugged. "Flattery gets me second helpings."

Grams swatted his butt with a dishtowel. "Scram. Both of you."

I followed Kerry down the path to the dock. "That's a nice boat you have," I said. I wasn't being sarcastic; at that point, any boat with a motor was a cruise ship to me.

Kerry shrugged. "She gets me where I'm going."

"No one in Springdale has their own boat," I added, impressed. Not that anyone had much use for one; Springdale Creek was less than twenty feet across.

"This boat's not my own either. It was my dad's."

"Your dad bought a new one?" I asked, remembering the boat dealership I'd spotted in Wawa that first evening.

"My father's dead."

Oh. "Sorry," I said. "I didn't mean to—"

Kerry waved off my concern and bent down to pull two life vests from a milk crate in the boat. That's when I noticed for the first time the angry scars criss-crossing his shorts-clad legs.

"Here," he said, turning to toss me a life vest. "Put this on and take the seat up front."

"Does your boat have a name?" I asked. Boats in books and on TV always had names.

The motor sprang to life with one sharp pull. *"The She-Devil!"* Kerry yelled up to me. "Named after my dear mother!"

It was too loud out there on the water for actual conversation, but every few minutes, Kerry slowed the engine and pointed to people and spots of interest along the shoreline.

" . . . That's the Granger cottage. Fred Granger has a Newfoundland dog that swam all the way to the village to get Doc Will when Fred fell and broke his tailbone hiking on the north shore. Hal—that's short for 'halitosis'—got a special medal from the RCMP. I guess good deeds make up for bad breath.

" . . . Oh, there's Lucy Woodley in her garden. Give her a wave. She's eighty-six. Sunbathes nude on her dock every morning between nine and ten. When I was eleven, my buddies and I checked her out with binoculars. I had nightmares for a week.

" . . . See that stone mansion behind the pines? The Tinkers live there. Disgustingly rich, reclusive folk from Montreal. New to the lake this year. They're related somehow to the Trudeaus. Or is it Celine Dion? Well, in any case, they aren't related to *me.*

" . . . We're almost at the Marrotts'. I won't explain about their house. You'll see for yourself."

Oh. My. God. The Marrotts' small cottage was shingled with aluminum pop cans—thousands and thousands of them. The winding path leading from the dock to their front door was a multi-colored mosaic of chipped tiles and broken china set in cement. From every tree within a fifty-foot radius of the house hung cut-up milk cartons and bleach bottles filled with bird seed.

Kerry cut the engine and whispered, "When we go inside, check out the furniture. It's papier-mâché. All of it." He hoisted a huge cardboard box onto one shoulder. His legs seemed unsteady under the weight, but he brushed off my offer to help.

"What are you delivering?" I asked.

"Out-dated catalogues," he replied, leading the way up the porch steps. He barged right into the cottage and beckoned me to follow him into the kitchen. "Come on in. They're expecting me."

A stocky woman about fifty and a thin man with a shock of white curly hair were perched on thick papier-mâché stools in front of a brightly-painted papier-mâché table. They glanced up from where they were working on a laptop and waved.

Kerry plunked his delivery on the floor. "Hi Jack, Dorothy." He pointed to me. "This is Charlie."

Dorothy smiled brightly and reached a hand out for me to shake. "Nice to meet you."

Kerry walked over to the table and peered over Jack's shoulder. "The July newsletter?"

Jack beamed. "It's coming along splendidly. We were just polishing an article promoting the use of condensed chicken excrement to fuel farm equipment." He turned to me; I quickly hid my smirk. "Dorothy and I publish a monthly recycling newsletter for the region," he explained. "We're co-captains of the Triple R Society."

"Reduce, reuse, recycle," Dorothy chanted and rose so I could admire her handmade patchwork dress. "I know it's not haute couture, but it's functional."

Gotta make myself one of those, I thought. If necessary, I could wear it to Mike's and Barb's wedding. Barb would be mortified. It might make the whole ordeal worthwhile for me.

"Thanks for bringing the old catalogs over, Kerry," Dorothy said. "Papier-mâché fruit bowls make such wonderful Christmas gifts."

"Christmas? In June?" he asked.

"We like to get an early start. And *now* is when Sears is clearing out their the catalogs. I'd hate to see all that lovely paper go to waste. Here's something for your trouble, Kerry." She pulled a fifty-dollar bill from her dress pocket and passed it over. Kerry waved it off, said it was too much, *way* too much, but Dorothy gave him a sharp look and shoved the bill into his fist. She told him quietly that it was good to see him home again, that she knew he'd put the money to good use.

Home from where? I wondered.

Kerry sputtered thanks and stuffed the money in his pocket.

Jack eyed me with curiosity. "You're a summer girl?" he asked.

"I guess. I'm Josie Parson's granddaughter. I'm visiting until Labour Day weekend."

Jack stared at me a moment, then lurched happily off his stool for a better look. "Then you must be Geri's girl!"

Dorothy broke into a gigantic grin. "I *knew* you looked familiar."

"You knew my mother?" I asked.

Dorothy chuckled. "Of course. She babysat our twins for years. Before we gave up our car—bad for the environment— Jack and I used to drive to Wawa every Thursday night for dinner with friends. Delightful girl, Geri was. Baked gingerbread cookies with Scott and Sammy. Took them on nature hikes to collect pine cones for crafts. We always knew she'd be a wonderful mother. It's so sad, her getting sick and passing on so young."

Resentment gnawed at the pit of my stomach. People at Lake Ringrose talked about my mother like she died last week, not thirteen years ago. They had all these wonderful memories to draw from when all I had at home was a shoe box stuffed with keepsakes and that "book" Geri'd illustrated of my pre-school stories.

After a few more minutes of chitchat, Kerry and I excused ourselves so the Marrotts could get back to work. Jack told us to grab Cokes on our way out; he was eager to collect enough empty cans to shingle a new boathouse by Thanksgiving.

We relaxed on the dock with our drinks. Though Kerry sat less that three feet from me, he seemed miles away, lost in thought.

I didn't mean to stare, but my eyes were drawn once again to the scars on Kerry's legs.

"My father and I were in a snowmobile crash last winter," he said. "Dad died at the scene. I crushed my pelvis and both legs, busted an arm and my collarbone, smashed my ribs all to shit. I was discharged just last week from a rehab center in Sault Ste. Marie."

"I'm so sorry about your dad."

Kerry shrugged. "Yeah, well, it's history now."

Not likely. I couldn't see Kerry's eyes under the sunglasses he'd slipped back on, but I'd heard the catch in his voice.

"I'd be a mess if something happened to my dad," I said. "He's all I have."

"Your parents are divorced?"

"My mother died when I was three."

"Accident?"

I shook my head. "She had cancer."

The awkward silence that followed was broken when a bright flash at the very end of a long line of year-round properties caught my attention.

There it was again.

"What *was* that?" I asked, nudging Kerry's arm.

"What?"

"Over there." I pointed. Another flash.

"Weird. No one stays at Birch Point in the summer." Kerry checked his watch. "Let's go check it out."

I rose and began to crush my empty pop can. Kerry grabbed my wrist. His palm was warm and dry and rough. A shiver ran up my spine. Too much sun, Charlie, I told myself. First you see light flashes; now you're feeling . . . what *are* you feeling?

Kerry was unaffected. "Don't dent the can." He plucked it from my hand, rinsed it in the lake, and tossed it into a sturdy metal bin beside the dock. "Jack can't use it if it's squashed."

Shaking off my goose bumps, I climbed back aboard *The She-Devil.* Kerry revved the engine and we sped along the shore to where I'd seen the flashes of light.

"Brian Baker owns this property," Kerry told me.

"Brian Baker?"

"You've never heard of Brian Baker? He's a hotshot wildlife painter. Lives in New York now; wildlife painting is all the rage there, according to Lisa, who thinks she knows everything. Brian only comes to Lake Ringrose for a few weeks each spring and fall—to sketch, paint, do whatever artists do. He keeps to himself. He keeps away from *my family* in any case."

"Why's that?"

He shrugged. "I'm not sure. When I was a little kid, two or three, my father used to look after this place for Brian—cutting the grass and repairing weather damage mostly; I sort of remember bouncing around with him on the riding mower. But I guess Brian and my father had some kind of falling out—over what I don't know. Payment, probably. They steered clear of each other after that."

"This place doesn't look like it's seen a lawn mower in years," I remarked.

Kerry looked around, nodding. "Brian lets the place go to rot now. Doc Will says he packed out his paintings and valuables years ago to discourage break-ins and just brings whatever supplies he needs each time he comes."

We trudged up a steep embankment and through a thick stand of birch trees. In a small clearing stood a tiny log cabin.

"Pretty basic digs for a famous artist," I said. But then I noticed the view over the lake. It was worth millions. Or at least well worth the climb. At least for me; while I oohed and aahed, Kerry leaned against a tree massaging his thighs.

Kerry shook out his legs and frowned at me. "Wipe the concern off your face. I'm fine. Let's see if we can get inside."

"Isn't trespassing a crime?"

"We're not trespassing; we're just neighbors concerned about some light flashes. Things are different around here, Charlie-girl," he said.

"Different from where?" Like he would know?

Kerry scowled. "Different from Wawa. Different from Sault Ste. Marie. Different from anywhere that you phone 911 and emergency services come running. I do travel out of the woods from time to time, you know."

"Sorry."

"All I meant is that Lake Ringrose looks after itself." He paused. "Well . . . at least most of the time."

"Kerry, what if someone *is* here?" I asked. "Someone with a guard dog. Or a rifle."

"I told you; Brian never comes here in the summer."

"Then what—or who—was making those flashes?" I suddenly felt chilled, and not just because the sun had ducked behind a cloud. "This house isn't built on a native burial ground or something, is it?"

"Don't start talking tourist trash," Kerry groaned, then continued to survey the property. "It's definitely not a fire. There doesn't seem to have been an explosion." He pointed to the roof and laughed. "Look up there. The flashes were probably just the sun reflecting off those skylights."

"Maybe. Maybe not."

"Maybe *you've* just seen too many late night horror movies."

Yeah. The ones where unsuspecting teenagers traipse into the woods to investigate strange noises or mysterious lights and meet up with angry weapon-wielding psychopaths.

Kerry climbed up the porch steps and rapped on the door. No answer. He tried the knob. Locked. He peered through a window. "Everything looks fine. No dead bodies lying in plain view."

How comforting. "What's down that path?" I asked, pointing to a narrow gap in the trees to the side of the cabin.

"Ladies first."

"No way."

Kerry made cluck-cluck chicken noises and set off through the trees. I trudged after him. No way was I going to be left behind. Alone.

The path ended a few hundred feet later in another small clearing.

"It's just an old barn," Kerry said.

We circled the building and I noticed a row of large windows on the north-facing wall, much newer than the old barn itself. "Maybe it's Brian Baker's art studio?" I suggested. I'd read something about artists preferring indirect light.

Kerry tried the main door; it was padlocked. But a garage-type hatch at the back of the barn swung up part way on creaky hinges. He motioned me to duck inside.

"I don't know."

"Where's your sense of adventure?"

"I was born without one. Chromosomal abnormality."

"You're not afraid of *me*, are you?" Kerry asked, like it had only just occurred to him that daring Josie Parson's granddaughter to accompany him into a deserted old barn might be a stupid idea.

"You wish." I smirked and ducked under the hatch, Kerry on my heels, only to be encased by a net of spider webs. Brushing the sticky threads from my hair—and stifling the urge to run back outside—I gazed through dusty sunbeams at a large open area, empty except for a pile of rusted antique farm equipment thick with dust. Leftovers from another era, a previous owner. "Prime ghost real estate," I mumbled.

Kerry wandered towards the front of the barn, where a large space had been partitioned with drywall into several small rooms. "Charlie?" He beckoned me to one of the doorways with his hand. "You've got to see this."

I peered around Kerry's shoulder, and sucked in my breath. The tiny room was empty except for a dusty futon. But the walls were incredible. A boreal forest mural, complete with several lifelike—life-*sized!*—moose, spanned all four walls. The plank floor had been painted too, with rocks and wildflowers and squirrels. Even the ceiling sported acrylic clouds and Canada geese in formation.

"Imagine sleeping in this room!" Kerry exclaimed. "It would be like camping every night, only without the bugs."

Think of the *nightmares*. Waking up every morning with those big moose in your face.

Kerry continued admiring the details of the painting while I poked into a sparse kitchen area containing a table, one chair, an electric kettle, and an empty mini-fridge. Beside it was—I was right—Brian's studio, complete with a crusty sink, a long work table, and several stools and paint-stained easels stacked neatly against one wall. The room smelled of old turpentine, though no paints, brushes, or other art supplies had been left behind, except . . .

High above the sink was a shelf, bare except for a long row of dusty art textbooks and what I recognized—from my own feeble attempts at art in junior high—as a basic black sketchbook. Curious to see more of Brian's artwork, I surreptitiously glanced around for a hidden camera, then, satisfied that there wasn't one, I gingerly took the book down for a peek.

To the cover was affixed a strip of yellowed masking tape. On the tape was written a name, in black ink now faded to gray, in small, loopy script similar to my own.

Geraldine Parsons.

My breath caught in my throat. My knees wobbled. The floor began to tilt.

Then a firm hand on my shoulder. "What did you find?" Kerry asked.

"It's a sketchbook," I replied. "It belonged to my mother."

Chapter Ten

Kerry and I arrived back at Grams' minutes before six, the sketchbook tucked under my sweatshirt. I felt like a thief, but Kerry convinced me that taking something that rightfully—well, *probably*—belonged to Grams and me wasn't really stealing.

Grams met us at the door. "Your mother called for you, Kerry."

"How did she know I was here?"

"Mother's intuition, I guess."

"What did she want?"

"Just to know if you were off somewhere seducing my granddaughter."

I scowled. Why were Grams and Jenny so suspicious about Kerry and I hooking up? So he was older. So it was "difficult being a teenager" at Lake Ringrose, as my grandmother put it, whatever she was implying. Maybe I had no experience when it came to boyfriends, and maybe Kerry had great lips and his hand on my arm had given me the shivers, but I was quite sure that he *hadn't* been putting the moves on me. *And so what if he did?* It's not like I was eleven years old. It's not like I had the looks and personality that had guys lining up to ask me out. If Kerry was showing an interest, he should be getting a public service award, not hassles. "Anyhow," Grams added, "she wants you home for dinner. Your favorite: fried liver and broccoli."

Kerry stuck a finger in his throat and made retching noises. Very mature.

Shaking her head, Grams filled a thermal jug with three heaping scoops of chili. She tossed two corn muffins in a paper bag. The whole works was thrust at Kerry's chest. "Our secret."

He got down on one rickety knee and took Grams' hand. "Josie, will you marry me?"

She laughed and helped Kerry back to his feet. "Watch out, kid. One of these days I might say yes."

With his care package clutched in his arms, Kerry backed out the screen door and retraced his steps to the dock. Grams turned to me, grinning. "Dinner time. Go change out of your damp clothes while I dish out the grub."

When I first arrived at Lake Ringrose, I thought it would be spooky sleeping in a room that, at first glance, seemed to have been kept as a shrine to my dead mother. But it wasn't. Truthfully, the small back bedroom was more of a hands-on museum exhibit showcasing the pop culture of the 1980s. Each morning, I woke in a time warp.

There were lots of framed musician posters. A teenage Madonna in a ripped lace dress and gloves. Michael Jackson, before he cut his nose off. Duran Duran. Boy George. Men At Work—they were Australian, I knew; staring at that poster, feelings for Sam would sometimes wash over me like a white squall. There were movie posters, too: *Flashdance, Tootsie, The Breakfast Club, Back To The Future, Rambo. Rambo?* My mother liked *Rambo?*

jrist

73

Though Grams said I was welcome to poke through whatever I liked, I felt like a snoop rummaging through Geri's drawers and closets. I wouldn't want anyone back home rifling though *my* drawers and closets, even if I *were* dead. It wasn't like I collected contraband; I just took my privacy for granted.

But feeling like a snoop didn't stop me from snooping. In Geri's drawers, I discovered a vintage Sony Walkman, a vast collection of battered music cassettes and VHS movies, a jewelry case full of dangly silver earrings, and a well-worn pair of what are now called "retro" Nike runners, size seven, same as me. The closet was stuffed with books, not clothes—Grams said she and Gramps had given what outfits Geri left behind when she went to university to a homeless charity in Wawa. There were hundreds of books: picture books, Nancy Drews, the *Lord of the Rings* trilogy, vast rows of paperback romances and science fiction, and neat piles of non-fiction books— everything from art and astronomy to zoology. There were magazines, too: *Tiger Beat,* with Kirk Cameron and Michael J. Fox on the cover. *Seventeen,* with big-haired cover models wearing pink corduroy jackets, patterned leg warmers, and neon gloves with no fingers.

My snooping had a purpose. I wanted to see if, unlike me, my mother had kept a diary or journal or some other record of her life, something from which I could derive information about who she'd been, what she'd felt, where she was in her head when she was sixteen. I'd wanted a tool, I suppose, against which to gauge my own level of intelligence, or maturity, or perhaps sanity.

I didn't find one.

But now I had the sketchbook.

I slipped it under the mattress and changed into clean shorts and a sweatshirt. Running a brush through my wind-blown tangles, I regarded my face closely in the mirror and considered how many times my mother had gazed into this same mirror. Wondered if she'd seen much the same reflection. Supposed that she, too, had had some days when she just wanted to stick her tongue out at herself.

I didn't really believe in ghosts or the supernatural or hocus pocus, but I couldn't get the flashes of light I'd seen that afternoon out of my head. Was it really the sun reflecting off Brian Baker's skylights—that was the logical, scientific explanation—or was it my mother, Geri, beckoning me to retrieve her sketchbook?

And if so, why?

After our chili feast, Grams went to the den to watch *Wheel of Fortune* and *Jeopardy* on her TV—in Lake Ringrose, satellite dishes are part of the family, Grams told me once, laughing.

I left the dishes on the rack to drip dry, fetched the sketchbook, and snuck out to the screened porch. Curled up on the swing, with cricket chirps and loon calls providing the soundtrack, I took a deep breath, opened the book's dusty cover, and began what Mr. Pollen would probably describe as "an exploration of my mother's artistic psyche."

She didn't disappoint. The sketchbook was thick, 200-plus pages, over half full of pencil sketches, ink drawings, and watercolors, some dating all the way back to the late seventies, when Geri was only in seventh or eighth grade. There were pencil portraits of people from the lake: Grams and Gramps on the hammock; a much-younger Doc Will, standing proudly beside his bush plane; small twin boys—the

Marrott kids?—eating ice cream cones. There were watercolors of puppies, squirrels, raccoons, sunrises, and a mammoth tree house nestled between the thick, slanted trunks of three tall pines.

My mother was using that same sketchbook two years later when she first met Mike at Camp Kanusabi, even though Mike always insisted that Geri hated his guts that summer. But there it was, a pastel sketch of a short boy in ragged cut-offs and glasses, with the big nose and lopsided grin that yelled "Mike." Underneath the sketch, in pink pencil crayon, Geri had drawn a little heart with "GP loves MC" printed inside. Had Mike ever seen this? Seeing it now would throw him for a loop, that was for sure.

"Where on earth did you find that?"

I'd been so absorbed in the sketches, I hadn't heard Grams step out onto the porch.

She handed me a mug of hot chocolate. I scootched over so she could sit beside me. "I used to wonder whatever happened to that sketchbook. I assumed Mike had it."

Caught with the goods, I spilled the whole truth, explaining to Grams about Kerry and I checking out the light flashes at Birch Point. Grams said that we were right to investigate and agreed with Kerry that the flashes probably *had* just been the sun on Brian's skylights. If Grams was upset about Kerry and I trespassing in Brian Baker's studio she didn't say; she was too excited about seeing the drawings again. Instead of being concerned about my "stealing," she seemed to think I'd reclaimed a treasure.

"Geri must have left the sketchbook behind the last time she tutored with Brian. He probably set it aside thinking she'd come back for it someday, then simply forgot about it.

He doesn't socialize much with the villagers when he visits Lake Ringrose. He might not even know that Geri died."

"Geri tutored with Brian?"

Grams nodded. "She had it in her head that she wanted to be a famous artist one day."

News to me. I knew my mother was artistic, but I'd never known she wanted to make a career of it. Nailed to the porch railing was a small framed pen and ink drawing of a chipmunk eating a peanut. "She did that?" I pointed.

Grams nodded again. "That was Charlie the chipmunk. Your mother tamed him to hunt for peanuts in her pockets."

"I was named after a *chipmunk*? Did I look like a rodent when I was born?"

"You were beautiful."

That didn't answer my question, but whatever. "So why did my mother become a nurse?"

"It's a long story."

I waited.

Grams took a sip of her hot chocolate. "Well, when she was your age, Geri wanted to become an illustrator or designer. She even sent away for a truckload of brochures about art colleges. And when Brian Baker moved into that old cabin at Birch Point the autumn of her senior year, your mother couldn't have been more excited if Mel Gibson had come to town. Geri begged him to tutor her. He looked through her sketchbook and agreed she could come over to his studio every Wednesday after school let out. He didn't want payment; he said it would be a pleasure to help her 'realize her potential,' as he called it."

"So what happened?" I asked.

"I'm not sure. Things seemed to be going so well at first. Geri couldn't stop singing his praises. When I ran into

Brian at the post office one morning, he told me Geri had great talent."

"But?" Wasn't there always a *but?*

"But . . . since Geri hadn't any formal art training, Brian was going to try to tighten up some of her rough areas. Encourage her to push beyond her comfort zones. Try some new things, and—"

Oh. That.

"—Geri got frustrated with the new things—the perspective and stippling techniques and what all; they didn't come as naturally to her as freeform drawing did."

Or maybe Brian and Mr. Pollen graduated from the same Nasty Old Coots School of Tactless Criticism, I wondered.

"Anyhow," Grams continued, "Geri came home one day all in a lather. She didn't want to talk about what Brian had said to upset her. She just closed up like a clam. Then a few days later she burned all her art school brochures in the fireplace and told me that she'd decided to pursue a more practical career. Nursing."

Well. So besides Geri's wide hips, crazy hair, and sense of humor, I'd also inherited her short fuse and what Mr. Pollen liked to call "my defensive posture." I didn't need to ponder about what other genetic surprises might be in store for me; worries about cancer had coursed through my brain like an undercurrent for years.

Grams sighed. "Maybe I should have tried harder to find out what was bothering Geri, but to be honest, I didn't encourage her artwork as much as I should have."

"How come?" I frowned, thinking of all Mike's kudos for my writing, whether I deserved them or not. I could write him a grocery list and he'd find something to praise about it.

"I knew succeeding as an artist would be a hard road," Grams replied. "Nursing was a sure thing. Geri even said that she might like to come back to the lake after her schooling to assist Doc Will. But as you know, she hooked up with Mike at university and that was that. True love. Your grandfather and I were shocked when Geri announced that she was getting married and starting a life in Springdale. But once I met Mike, I knew Geri'd snagged herself a keeper."

Mike a *keeper?* Balding, pudgy, work-a-holic Mike? "What was it about Mike she fell in love with?" I asked, bewildered. I knew Barb loved him for his ability to construct IKEA furniture and eagerness to play air hockey with the boys while she got her hair done, but I liked to think that my mother had higher standards.

"Geri always said that Mike's laugh was contagious. And that he was smart and kind and responsible; in her words, 'so different from Greg Sanderson'."

"Greg Sanderson?"

"Just a local boy she pined for when she was a teenager. He played her along for awhile—her and all the other girls in the village—but finally settled on Jenny Chambers."

"You mean Jenny from the café? Kerry's mother?"

Grams nodded. "Jenny and Greg married about a year after your mother left for university." She paused. "Greg died last winter."

"Kerry told me they were in a snowmobile accident."

"Kerry was lucky to survive."

I wondered if Kerry felt so "lucky." "How did it happen?" I asked.

Grams shot me an I-probably-shouldn't-tell-you-this look, then told me anyway. "It was New Year's Eve, very late, snowing.

Greg and Kerry both knew damn well not to take a snowmobile onto the lake that early in the winter; the ice here can't be trusted until mid-January. They hit a boulder. Kerry was thrown onto a solid ice patch—thank God. Greg and the snowmobile went right through the ice." Grams' angry eyes told me there was more to it, *a lot more*, but she wouldn't elaborate.

"The village must have been horrified," I said. Every few years, a tragedy struck Springdale, too: creek drownings during the spring thaw, fires caused by careless smoking, teenagers running their parents' cars into telephone poles on prom night . . . infamous creative writing teachers having heart attacks in the grocery checkout line.

"Unfortunately, Greg's death *didn't* come as a shock," Grams huffed. "He was an accident waiting to happen. Don't get me wrong, Charlena; Greg Sanderson wasn't without his good points, but he never grew up."

Grams looked me in the eye. "He never learned to take responsibility for his actions."

Grams and I sat together on the porch swing for over an hour, flipping through the sketchbook. Grams was able to identify the subjects of most of the drawings and told me little stories about each one.

When she excused herself for bed, I continued exploring the book, studying the artwork as if for a test, trying to get a feel for the teenage girl who created it. I liked that Geri drew only things she cared deeply about: family, friends, animals, familiar places. There were no fruit bowls or other "arrangements," no movie star portraits or cartoon superheroes.

Unfamiliar handwriting was scrawled across what appeared to be the final series of sketches. On a detailed pen and ink rendering of Grams' house: *"Excellent perspective, but not enough contrast. Too dark!"* On a stippled drawing of an old fishing boat washed aground: *"Technically sound, but you failed to capture the spirit of the subject matter."* The final piece, a watercolor of a deer eating twigs: *"You are capable of better."*

I flipped a few more pages. They were blank.

I could just imagine Geri telling Brian where to shove his tutoring and slamming off home, forgetting to collect her belongings. And I could see how Geri might have let Brian's criticism get to her—the drawings were fantastic. I couldn't draw to save my life; even my stick people were deformed.

But I saw some other things, too.

I turned back to the sketch of Grams' house. True, it was a little dark, as if it depicted the house at dusk. But maybe that's what Geri had intended. Who cared if it might look better with more light reflected off the windows? A greeting card company? A gallery owner?

And the fishing boat, while technically perfect, *was* missing something I couldn't put my finger on. Old fishing boats tell stories about the places they've been, the crews they've carried, but Geri's boat was silent. Its hull held no secrets, nothing that would make you want to stare at it over the fireplace for hours at a stretch.

By contrast, the watercolor of the hungry deer had character to spare. The animal seemed to be almost smirking at me, daring me to find as much pleasure as he did chewing a mouthful of twigs. Okay, so there was something a little cartoony—*Bambi*-ish—about the eyes, but it wasn't something that couldn't be tweaked.

Thinking back to the paintings Geri had done for our "book," I realized I'd never looked at them with a critical eye, only the eyes of a kid who had those paintings instead of mother-daughter memories. I saw the love in the paintings, not the mistakes. It was like Mike with my stories, I realized. He wouldn't recognize great writing if the words jumped off the page and bit him on the ass, but he knew what was important to me and he supported it, encouraged me, praised my stories even when they needed nothing short of CPR. He built me up, only leaving me to be toppled by the likes of Hector Pollen and his highfalutin professional opinions. Did Grams do Geri a favor by not encouraging her artistic ambitions?

"No, she didn't!" a voice inside my head screamed. Who *was* that? Was I going schizophrenic, or was I just changing my mind? It had been so long since I re-thought anything.

Okay, so maybe my mother shouldn't have let Grams and Brian Baker kill her dreams of being an artist. But maybe they didn't kill her dreams at all; maybe Geri's dreams just changed one day. But why then was her artwork the thing she chose to leave me before she died? Geri didn't spend her last months knitting me sweaters or gardening or watching the old TV sitcoms Mike said she used to love. With time running out, my mother *chose* to illustrate my stories. Her paintings weren't just art, they were a message. Geri wanted me to never forget that she loved me.

Was there was a message for me in the sketchbook, too?

Chapter Eleven

Mike phoned the next day to check in. He and Barb were leaving for Toronto the next morning. "Well," he asked. "How's it going?"

I explained about learning to paddle a canoe, the dubious thrills of scraping twenty-year-old paint blisters off wooden shingles, and picking wild strawberries behind Grams' storage shed. I reported seeing a white-tailed deer across the lake through Grams' high powered binoculars. I tattled about how Grams had made me drive her car all the way from Wawa to Lake Ringrose, expecting/hoping him to be mortified with worry. Instead, Mike said, "That's great, Char! So I guess you'll stick it out there for the summer?"

"Whatever." I couldn't leave now, anyway; the outside of Grams' house was only one-quarter painted and we hadn't even chosen colors for the kitchen and living room. The place really did need a tremendous amount of work. Grams needed my help. And *I* needed to be needed for a change.

"You can change your mind anytime, Char. It's probably too late for the camp job, but you're always welcome to join me and Barb in Toronto."

Yeah, Mike. You and Barb and I cramped into a one-bedroom faculty sub-let. How cozy. How positively hive-inducing. "You don't miss me already, do you?" I asked, joking.

"Of course I miss you."

"Not as much as you'd miss your computer and fax machine if they disappeared for the summer."

I'd stabbed him. "Char, you know that's not true."

I don't know what made me say stuff like that to Mike sometimes. I may have resented his round-the-clock work habits—not to mention his recent trade-in of our already limited father-daughter time for a love life—but at least I usually knew where to find him in a pinch. Not every kid could say that about his or her father.

Mike changed the subject. "Char, Sam called this morning."

I must have heard wrong. *"Sam?"*

"All the way from Australia. He was worried, said he hasn't received an e-mail from you in almost two months. Is that true?"

Kaboom. Ka-ka-boooom. Kabobobooboom. My heart thumped like a first grader on the bongos. It was all I could do not to drop the phone. "I was busy, Mike. Finals and all. Packing for my trip."

Mike didn't buy it. "Are you upset with him for some reason?"

"No," I lied.

"He's your best friend, Char. You know he cares about you a great deal if he phoned all that distance just to see if—"

"No," I insisted. "I'm not upset."

"Well, I gave him your address up at Lake Ringrose and let him know you left your computer at home, so not to send or expect e-mail. You have Sam's mailing address, right? Send him a note, Char. He sounded homesick. I'm sure moving to Australia has been quite a difficult adjustment for him."

Bullshit. "I'm really quite busy, Mike," I sighed. "But I'll try."

Mike didn't pursue it further. He'd get frostbite in hell before I'd tell him I did a stupid thing like tell Sam I loved him. Confess I struck out, romantically speaking, my first time at bat. Admit that Sam was in cahoots with an "Elizabeth" now.

But Sam had called. He was *worried* about me. I grinned into the phone receiver despite myself.

Mike introduced an equally uncomfortable subject. "Just so you know, Char, I was talking to Paul Cozza down the street this morning; he'll be cutting the lawn and forwarding my mail to Toronto this summer. He heard that Hector Pollen is still in the hospital. His surgery was successful, but he may have contracted pneumonia. Sorry. I was hoping to have better news for you."

I closed my eyes. I couldn't speak. I was glad Mr. Pollen was still alive, but horrified that things were still touch and go. And did I want Mr. Pollen to live so that I could buck up, reaffirm my writing aspirations, and once again subject myself to his harsh editorial criticisms? Or did I just want to not feel guilty for the rest of my life for being rude to a man with a weak heart?

"Char, you there?"

"I'm okay."

"I sent a plant to the hospital. I signed your name."

Mr. Pollen didn't want a plant from me. He wanted my blood, my soul, a flawless writing assignment.

"Thanks," I said.

"Listen, Char. Barb's beeping through," Mike said. "I'll phone again when I reach Toronto."

"Have fun in the city. Send me a postcard from the dome." I took a deep breath and made his day. "And tell Barb I said hi."

Chapter Twelve

One evening a week or so later, I was in the bedroom folding laundry when my peripheral vision picked up movement outside the window.

I turned—and screeched!

Grams came running from the bathroom where she'd been putting her hair in curlers. "What is it? What now!"

It was Kerry, hanging from a small tree by one arm, hooting like an owl.

I slid open the window. "What the hell are you doing out there?"

"Hey, you. I was trying to catch your attention."

"Ever heard of knocking on the door?"

Kerry dropped a few inches to the ground, grimacing only slightly, and sauntered over to the window. He seemed more sure on his feet tonight, not so much like he was walking on stilts. "And miss hearing you carry on like that? You play tough, Charlie-girl, but you're a total marshmallow."

"That's me, the human Jet Puff."

"Actually, I'm on my way to the pond to collect bait. I've got the ATV and a spare helmet. How about it?"

Grams grinned. "You asking me?"

Kerry laughed. "Be tough for you to fit the helmet over all those curlers, Josie. I'll have to settle for Charlie." He turned to me. "So?"

"What exactly does 'collecting bait' entail?"

"Digging for worms and slugs. Checking minnow traps."

"I don't think I'm cut out for that."

"It's the twenty-first century, Charlie-girl; don't go suggesting that slug-digging is a man's job."

I snuck a look at Grams. Well? It was barely eight-thirty. What else was I going to do that night besides shave my legs and pick latex paint out of my cuticles?

Grams seemed light years away.

"Grams?" I hoped she wasn't getting Alzheimer's or something.

She snapped out of it. "Okay, Charlena. But don't be too long. It smells like rain."

"I'll take care of your precious cargo," Kerry assured Grams.

I sneered. *"Precious Cargo* can take care of herself."

Kerry led me over to where he'd parked his muddy, oversized, four-wheeled motorcycle behind Grams' station wagon.

"All-terrain vehicles are great on the back trails. I won this baby three years ago in a hockey raffle. Want to drive it?" he asked me.

What was next? Flying a bush plane? Manning a hot air balloon? "Sure," I replied. I'd show Kerry I wasn't such a marshmallow. Besides, *Charlie Conroy: Biker Chick* had a nice ring to it. I straddled the seat, making "vroom, vroom" noises like a five-year-old. "If Sam could see me now," I chuckled under my breath.

Kerry tossed me his spare helmet. "Who's Sam? Your brother?"

I shook my head. "Just a guy back home. He moved to Australia a few months ago."

"Was he your boyfriend?"

"NO!"

"No need to get defensive, Charlie-girl."

"Sam is just a friend."

Kerry gave me a smug grin. "Uh huh."

"Don't act like that," I said, annoyed.

"Like what?"

"Like you know better."

"Sorry," Kerry said. But he was grinning. Jerk.

"Sam is just a friend," I repeated. If I said it enough times, maybe I'd even believe it myself.

"You mean like a female friend?" Kerry asked.

"I don't have female friends," I admitted.

"Why not? You have some contagious social affliction Josie didn't warn me about?"

"Because I wear sneakers and baseball caps and my father's hand-me-downs to school. Because I don't wear makeup or nail polish or giggle over pictures of Ashton Kutcher in magazines at the 7-Eleven. Because all my life, my best friend has been a gawky, red-haired, computer-freak boy with a mouthful of braces. Want to hear more?"

"No. I got the picture. You're a lesbian," Kerry said.

"*What!*"

"I'm just teasing. I know you aren't a lesbian."

"How do you know that?"

Kerry grinned. "I just know."

Shit. Did he notice me ogling his lips the other day?

"So," Kerry continued, "is this gawky, red-haired, computer-freak boy by any chance named Sam?"

"So?"

"So have you told him how bad you've got it for him?"

"I do not!"

"Does he know you can't even *hear* his name without blushing?"

"I do *not* blush."

"You know," Kerry said. "Lisa's boyfriend has—let me say this delicately—an *acne* problem. But she says that a guy who is smart and funny and nice, even if he looks like an English bulldog, is more attractive to her than any arrogant male model. Not that she knows any male models."

"Sam doesn't have 'an acne problem'," I growled. *"Nor does he look like an English bulldog."* Then I cracked a smile. "Okay, maybe he's a little like an Irish Setter puppy, what with his long legs, big feet, red whiskers."

"You've left out the floppy ears, cold nose, and housebreaking problem," Kerry snorted, then asked, "What kind of dog am I?"

"Hmm. If you were to press your face against a pane of glass, you'd look exactly like a boxer."

"You do know how to charm a guy, Charlie-girl."

I patted the ATV, eager to change the subject. "You gonna teach me to drive this thing or not?"

Kerry tightened my helmet—I didn't need a mirror to know it made me look like a large shiny-headed beetle—and gestured for me to scoot up a little on the seat. He plunked himself behind me. Leaning over my shoulder, he showed me where the ignition was and how to accelerate and apply the brakes. I barely paid attention; Kerry smelled like Coppertone and cinnamon Dentyne, and his stubbly cheek against my ear was giving me heart palpitations.

I grasped the ignition key in my sweaty fingers and took a deep breath. "Here goes."

The four-wheeler roared beneath us.

"Give it some juice!" Kerry shouted in my ear.

I juiced it. We shot forward. I braked. We stalled. I juiced it again. I braked again. *Hard.*

"I'm getting whiplash back here, Charlie-girl! Take it nice and easy," Kerry said, leaning over me again and putting his hands over mine. "Like this."

We took it nice and easy up Grams' lane and onto the main dirt road. When Kerry let go, I propelled us forward on my own, gaining confidence and then speed on the straightaway. The fresh pine air, the wind on my face, the roar of the horsepower beneath me . . . it was enough to make me forget that I was a surly teenager.

Was this grist?

Kerry gestured for me to stop at the turnoff onto a narrow, hilly trail. "I better take it from here."

We quickly switched positions. "Hang on tight," Kerry said. "It's going to get bumpy."

I dug my fingernails into the edge of the seat beneath me.

Kerry revved the ATV and we took off uphill. I jolted backwards. In fear, I forgot my shyness and wrapped my arms around Kerry's waist, locked my wrists, and held on for dear life.

Kerry yelled over his shoulder, "Not too tight! I had a big dinner. It's the wrong time to be practicing your Heimlich Maneuver."

I loosened my grip. Slightly.

The trail took us through a stand of tall pines, across a meadow of daisies, then along an overgrown lane littered with small, falling-down cabins Kerry told me had been used a hundred years ago by native hunters and trappers.

As the cool dusk approached, dark birds swooped down to feast on swarms of biting insects.

"What kind of birds are those?" I shouted in Kerry's ear.

"They aren't birds!" Kerry shouted back. "They're bats."

He was just pulling my chain, right? *Bats?*

"Yeah."

"Real bats? Get-tangled-in-your-hair bats? Suck-your-blood *vampire* bats?"

Kerry shrugged. "Just plain old brown bats."

I am tough, I thought. Well, I could pretend to be tough. What was that dumb affirmation Barb spouted all the time? Oh yeah: "Fake it 'til you make it."

Another ten minutes along an increasingly dark and wooded trail, Kerry brought the four-wheeler to a halt and pulled off his helmet. I removed mine, too, and tried not to think about what a fine nest my thick unruly hair would make for some homeless bat family. Kerry grabbed two flashlights from the ATV's small cargo hold. He passed one to me, then removed two big pails with lids and a collapsible shovel. "It's a bit of a hike to the pond," he said, steering me towards a narrow path through the forest.

"This isn't going to turn out like *The Blair Witch Project,* is it?" I asked.

"Hope not," Kerry said, then winked when he realized my apprehension was real. "Don't worry, Charlie-girl. I come out here to the pond almost every night."

Right, don't worry. *Don't worry???* There I was, on a Friday night, in the middle of God-knows-where, with a guy I barely knew, surrounded by bats and who knows what other night creatures, hiking to an alleged pond to collect bait. Was this, or was this not, an improvement over sitting alone on the couch back in Springdale, scarfing junk food, and watching old movies on cable?

Was *this* grist?

"So I guess you still fish a lot?" I asked the back of Kerry's head. The path wasn't wide enough for us to walk side by side.

"A little," he replied over his shoulder. "Pike and trout mostly. But the bait we collect tonight isn't for me. I sell it to the marina. The marina sells it to the summer cottagers."

Café sweeper. Delivery boy. Worm digger. Seemed Kerry, despite his injuries, was always doing something. "How many jobs do you have?" I asked.

"As many as I want. I'm not picky and not afraid to get my hands dirty. And Doc Will says that the exercise is good therapy for my legs." He paused. "Besides, working keeps me out of trouble."

I was tempted to ask what kind of trouble, but Kerry had picked up the pace. Maybe I'd asked enough questions for one night. I trotted silently behind him for the next five minutes and tried to ignore the sounds of the woods.

Tried.

Something howled in the distance.

"Was that a wolf?" I trotted closer and fought the urge to take hold of the back of Kerry's shirt for protection.

"It was probably just that dog Hal I told you about."

"Probably?"

"Or maybe it was a Bigfoot."

"Very funny, smart-ass. Are there wolves in this forest or not?"

Kerry glanced back at me. "One look at the scowl on your wimpy town-girl face and they'd pack up the pups and head for Thunder Bay."

"You didn't answer my question!"

Kerry shook his head in exasperation. "Yes. There are wolves in this forest. Happy now?"

"Ecstatic."

Five more minutes along the trail, Kerry stopped so suddenly that I walked right into him. We'd arrived at the pond, oval-shaped and no larger than a regulation hockey rink. In the wide beam of my flashlight, I spotted more than a dozen birch saplings that had been felled along the shore, their stumps whittled away to sharp points.

"Beavers," Kerry explained before I could ask. "This used to be a creek fifty years ago, before the beavers dammed up the south end. Engineers have learned a lot from beavers," he added knowingly. "I guess that's why it's Canada's national animal."

I shook my head. "It's not because of the dams, Kerry; it's that beaver pelts made such nice waterproof hats for the rich seventeenth-century Europeans. The fur trade opened up the interior of Canada and led to settlement across the country." At least according to Mr. Habib, my history teacher.

"Thank you for the tutorial, Miss Know-it-all," Kerry said, shaking his head. "You. Lisa. My mother. Thank God there are women in my life to remind me I'm an idiot." He set his flashlight on a rock and focused it at a patch of ground. Using the shovel, he turned over a patch of damp earth, exposing scores of squirming worms. "I don't know my history text, Charlie-girl," he added, "but I know worms. Catch," he said, tossing me a pail. "Fill it half-full with soil, then add a hundred worms. Try not to mutilate them or lose count. I'm going to check the minnow traps."

Thankfully for me, collecting live worms was a much less disgusting task than slicing apart dead ones in Biology. I sang loudly as I worked, an old camp song, to scare away the wildlife that I imagined were watching me. That were licking their chops in anticipation of having a tasty "wimpy town-girl" for dinner.

"Nobody loves me, everybody hates me, think I'll go eat worms—"

Kerry sidled up to me, his minnow bucket full. *"Big, fat juicy ones, little itty bitty ones—hey, shhhh—listen."*

The woods were alive. Leaves rustled in the wind, twigs snapped on the ground as small—*very small,* I prayed—animals scurried for shelter.

"Rain's coming," Kerry said, sealing the lid on his bucket.

Nature was bracing for a soaker. Within seconds, the rhythmic rustling in the distance became an insistent pitter-patter. A sudden stampede of water galloped up the trail towards Kerry and me.

"We're going to get drenched," Kerry said. "We need to get out of here."

I grabbed the flashlight and my bucket of worms intending to make a run for it back to the ATV.

"No!" Kerry shouted, stopping me in my tracks. "Fasten the lid on the bucket and leave it there for now. Bring your flashlight and come this way." He pointed towards the other side of the pond. "There's shelter." Taking his own flashlight in one hand and my hand in his other, he pulled me through the downpour around the muddy pond to a clump of tall pines.

The pines from my mother's sketchbook.

The pines supporting the tree house.

Chapter Thirteen

I shone my flashlight up between the slanted pine trunks. About thirty feet off the ground was a hut about twelve feet square made of a jumble of old plywood and used shingles. A sturdy aluminum ladder led up to a hatch in the floor.

Kerry motioned me to climb first. "We'll be safe up there. No lightning tonight."

I can do this, I thought. Hand, foot, hand, foot. Don't look down.

"Don't drop your flashlight on my head," Kerry said as he pulled himself up after me with a grunt.

Rain pelted the roof like bullets, but the tree house was dry and big enough for Kerry and me to maneuver. There was an air bed covered with a worn quilt in one corner, a couple of lawn chairs, boxes of jumbled clothing and cooking supplies, a kerosene lantern, a camp stove, and a locked metal box.

"Welcome to my nest," Kerry said, tossing me a dry towel.

"This tree house has been here for decades," I said, squeezing out my hair. "There's a watercolor of it in my mother's sketchbook."

Kerry lit the lantern and nodded. "My dad and his friends built it back when they were kids, but I've renovated. I put in a new floor and roof, fixed the leaks, replaced the ladder. My buddies and I used to skip school and hike out here to play cards and drink beer. This pond, and the trail we hiked through to get here, is my father's back lot. Mine and Lisa's back lot now, though Lisa insists she'll never live at Lake Ringrose again. Someday soon I want to clear a lane from the main trail and build a real cabin back here." He opened the metal box and showed me a cache of instant coffee, Kraft Dinner, hot chocolate mix, bottled water, Cokes, granola bars, Snickers, and packets of instant soup and oatmeal. "Want a Coke?" he asked.

I popped my Coke tab and plunked into a lawn chair. "So where are all your 'buddies' this summer, Kerry?" I was pretty sure that hanging out with the likes of me cramped his style.

Kerry settled into the other chair. "Some of the guys I used to run with graduated this year and got provincial park jobs down at Agawa Bay. A few others are doing construction work up in Marathon. I lost touch with most of them when I was away at rehab." He paused. "It's true what they say, you know."

"What is?"

"That a life-changing—*life-wrecking*—experience teaches you who your real friends are—*or aren't,* in my case. None of my buddies, *not one,* was willing to give up a weekend of wild partying to come down to Sault Ste. Marie and spend a not-so-wild weekend watching videos and eating pizza with a guy in a body cast. I had a girlfriend, too, from Wawa, who came down to see me once, then called the next day and broke up with me over the phone. She *said* it was because she needed to spend more time on her school work but I found out later that she'd told her friends that my injuries grossed her out.

That she thought I'd be paralyzed and in a wheelchair for the rest of my life. That I wouldn't be able to get it up anymore. I can, you know."

"Can what?" I asked stupidly.

"Get it up. Just in case you were wondering."

My usual smart-mouth comebacks deserted me. I wasn't comfortable talking sex with anyone, let alone a guy like Kerry, who may not have known his Canadian history, but probably knew at least as much about sex as he did about worms. It would take him about ten seconds to realize most eleven-year-olds had more experience than me.

I spied a guitar propped against the wall. "You play?" I asked.

"Sure." Kerry picked it up and strummed a few chords absently, then put it back down. "We're soaked through. Let me find a dry shirt first."

He rummaged through a cardboard box stuffed with clothes and pulled out a ratty green T-shirt and a heavy blue sweatshirt. As he stripped off his wet sweater and pulled the green T-shirt over his head, how could I not notice those chiseled shoulders and six-pack abs? Kerry's legs were a mess, but his chest could sell calendars.

He noticed me noticing and grinned. "I did a lot of swimming and weight-lifting in rehab. I've sort of kept up with it."

My face flamed. I hoped in the dim lantern light he wouldn't notice that, too.

"You're blushing again," he chided.

"I am not," I insisted.

"Here." Kerry tossed me the blue sweatshirt. It smelled like mothballs. "Take off your wet shirt and put that on."

What??? "I'm not taking my shirt off in front of you!"

"Don't get all embarrassed, Charlie-girl, but it's so wet right now I can see through it, anyway."

Horrified, I looked down and quickly crossed my arms over my chest.

"You want the shirt or not?" he asked.

"Well, turn your head and close your eyes!" I demanded.

Kerry chuckled and turned his back. I was out of my wet stuff and into the blue sweatshirt in five seconds flat.

"Done," I gasped.

"Nice breasts," Kerry commented.

I shrieked, *"You looked!"*

"I *peeked,*" Kerry admitted.

"You're a *PIG!*"

"I'm an eighteen-year-old guy; what did you expect?" Kerry laughed. "Besides, 'nice breasts' is a compliment, isn't it?"

"Like that makes it okay?"

"Would you rather I'd said you had funny-looking breasts?"

"I'd rather we not discuss my breasts at all."

"But it was okay for you to ogle my pecs?" Kerry asked, still clearly amused.

"Okay! Enough already!" I yelled, flinging my wet shirt over a beam to dry.

"Charlie-girl?"

"What?" I snapped.

"I didn't peek. I just wanted to get your goat."

I frowned, not willing to give Kerry the satisfaction of witnessing my relief. I got myself into this mess. What was I thinking, letting myself be led to a tree house in the woods, at night, in a rainstorm, with an older guy who may or may not have watched me undress? If this summer was a chapter

jrist

in my life, I wondered what Mr. Pollen would think of my plot and character development so far.

Kerry opened his food cache again and tossed me another warm Coke. "This just *seems* like a scene from *Friday the 13th.* I'm basically harmless."

"Basically? You've got enough rations in that box to harbor me here for weeks."

"Don't flatter yourself. It's just, since I got home from rehab, I've been pretty much living out here. Mom and I never got along at the best of times, and things have been more tense than usual these past couple weeks. I keep enough munchies on hand so that if I have to camp out here a few days at a time, I don't starve. I'm going to build that real cabin out here as soon as I can afford it." Kerry took a long swallow of Coke. "Dad and I had plans to lay the foundation this summer, but, well . . . "

I was a heel. Before I got my nose out of joint over the wet T-shirt issue, I'd been, well, enjoying myself. I couldn't remember a time I'd had fun just hanging out with someone who wasn't Sam. My attention fell on the guitar again. "Play me something, Kerry?"

"Well, I'm kind of a hack, but I—"

"Please?"

Kerry could blush, too. He started to blather. "Really? Well, there's this song I wrote when I was fourteen, right after my first real girlfriend dumped me for some dickhead summer guy with his own Jet Ski. I've never played it for anyone before, and it's real sappy, so—"

"Just play it," I said. "I'm your captive audience, aren't I?" I pointed to the roof where the rain continued to beat a steady rhythm. "You've even got a drummer."

Kerry took up the guitar again and began strumming. He cleared his throat a few times, then started singing. I'd been preparing to put on a show of enthusiasm even if his performance sucked, but he was . . . *wow!*

Sometimes I sit and wonder
What you and I once shared
Was it really just a few friendly smiles
Or could it be you really cared?

Sometimes I cry myself to sleep
Reminiscing of the past
Happy memories of yesterday
Why could we not last?

I will not forget the good old days
I will always be your friend
I want to make you smile and laugh again
It can't really be the end.

Sometimes I sit and wonder
What really happened and why
People are always changing
Maybe we could give it another try.

"Well?" Kerry set the guitar down and raised a skeptical brow. "You should try out for *Canadian Idol.*"

He scowled. "Don't be a smart-ass."

"I'm serious, Kerry," I said. "You're great. You've got it going on. Your voice is fabulous, you play guitar like a pro, *and* you wrote a song that people can relate to." Or that *I* could relate to anyway.

"Charlie-girl, were those honest-to-God *genuine* compliments that just slipped through your wise-cracking lips?"

"I won't even charge you for them."

"You really *liked* the song?" Kerry was incredulous.

"It was great. I love that one of us has a future as a writer."

Kerry balked. "I don't want to write songs for a living. The guitar is just something I mess around with when I'm bored."

"Oh," I said, deflating.

"*You* want to be a writer?" Kerry asked. "Let me guess, stand-up routines?"

Grrrrrrrrr. "I want—*wanted*—to write books. Novels. Great works of fiction!"

"Why?"

"*Why?*" No one had ever asked me "why." I'd just assumed the "why" was a given, that writing was a compulsion, not a choice. Something that I hoped could be treated with Prozac or painkillers if necessary. "Well," I stammered, "I've always liked the idea of taking risks on paper, constructing characters and putting them into situations that I might never attempt or experience in real life. It's like . . . if a fictional character screws up big time, or gets embarrassed, or hurt, no one in real life suffers. You know?"

"Sounds kind of cowardly," Kerry said.

"Writing is cowardly?"

"Not at all. But that reason is."

I could feel my hackles rising. Kerry was morphing into Mr. Pollen with pecs. I almost laughed at the image until I realized Mr. Pollen's pecs had been sliced open wide during his heart surgery. "Why is that, Kerry?" I choked.

"Think about it. You talk about creating this parallel storybook universe where people say and do the things you'd *like* to do in real life, but don't have the guts. Don't you think your writing would be stronger if you lived a little more outside your head, if you let yourself have a little fun and disaster in your life, then write about it?"

Yeah, like telling Sam I loved him. That was a smooth move, all right. Like coming to Lake Ringrose and finding that sketchbook that left me with more questions than answers about my mother. Like learning to paddle a canoe and drive an ATV and dig worms with the likes of Kerry. Grist-gathering was risky business. My heart wasn't closed to it, but my head was flashing neon warning signs: *Danger Ahead.*

The rain had been steadily subsiding. And it was getting late. I didn't want to stay and defend myself to Kerry, especially when I suspected he just might have been, despite his self-proclaimed "idiot" status, right. It's like he could see through me; not just through my shirt, but through my *skin.*

"Let's go." I gathered my still-wet shirt into a ball and started down the ladder before Kerry could stop me.

Using the flashlights to navigate, we traipsed through mud to the ATV and rode without words along the now-sloppy trail back to semi-civilization. When Kerry dropped me at Grams', I tossed him back his helmet and promised I'd get his sweater back to him someday soon. "Thanks for taking me along tonight," I added. "It was quite . . . uh . . . an adventure."

"Charlie-girl, what I said back there about your writing—I didn't mean to offend you."

"I'm not offended."

"Your body language says you are."

"Then stop looking at my body."

Kerry rolled his eyes. "I like you, kid."

"What's not to like?"

"Goodnight, Charlie-girl," he laughed, and quickly bent down and kissed my cheek.

I lifted my head, as if to return the kiss, but freaked out at the last nano-second. I bit the tip of Kerry's nose instead. Not hard—just a nibble really.

"Nighty-night, Kermit." I croaked and bolted across the lawn towards the porch stairs.

I could hear Kerry's laughter over the roar of the ATV as he drove back up the lane to the road. I could *still* hear him cackling in my head long after I'd entered the house. Thankfully, Grams had fallen asleep in her recliner and was oblivious to both the late hour and her granddaughter's indiscretions.

Am I insane? I wondered, as I stood in the bathroom brushing my teeth. Nothing in the eleventh-grade curriculum had prepared me for Nose-Nibbling 101. No wonder Grams warned me about Kerry. He was a guy with grist to spare. Stick with him awhile and who knew where my life would take me. What a terrifying concept. What a rush.

"And what about Sam?" that annoying voice in my head asked.

In bed, feeling an odd mixture of exhilaration and trepidation, I replayed the events of the past couple of weeks in my head. I almost wished that I had one of those reliable teen-novel girlfriends I could call for advice or analysis of the situation. I craved barbecue chips, but Grams didn't keep junk food in the house. So what was I to do?

I needed a way to capture my time at Lake Ringrose somehow, and I knew a postcard or souvenir bookmark

Heather Waldorf

104

wouldn't cut it. I flipped on a lamp, and for the first time since leaving Springdale, I dug the furry puppy journal out of my bag.

Chapter Fourteen

Early the next morning, Grams and I were back in the canoe. There was mail to pick up in the village.

"Want me to steer today?" I asked.

"Nah. Let the old lady do it."

Though she'd taught me the J-stroke and encouraged me to take daily paddles by myself along the shore, Grams always sterned when we went across the bay to the village. "You never know when some wacky summer cottager will come along in his powerboat and create a four-foot wake. I don't want to have to send you scuba-diving for my purse."

A wave of nostalgia washed over me. "When we were little, Sam and I wanted to be divers," I told Grams. "His family had a backyard pool. We'd wrap stones in foil and toss them in the water. Race to see who could collect the most before coming up for air."

"No place like Australia to go scuba-diving," Grams said. "Wouldn't it be wonderful if Sam got to visit the Great Barrier Reef?"

"Yeah, just wonderful." Another experience he'd get to share with "Elizabeth."

"You'll have wonderful experiences in your life, too, Charlena."

"Of course I will. Maybe next year Mike will get contracted to teach Accounting in South America; I can paddle the Amazon and learn to wrestle anacondas. Or maybe he'll take me to the Arctic Circle; I can harpoon seals and outrun polar bears. Or perhaps—"

Grams laughed. "Do you truly miss Sam's company, or are you just jealous that he gets to see the world this summer and you don't?"

Ouch.

She wasn't done. "Sam *lucked out*," she added, "by having a parent who was transferred overseas. It'll be up to you to create your own adventures, Charlena. There are an infinite number of opportunities out there for you. You just have to decide which ones you're willing to work for. You're young, smart, talented—"

"Grams, I think you've had too much sun."

"And I think you're all wet!" She splashed me with her paddle until I was drenched.

Okay, so sometimes Grams acted childish, but she also seemed wise about many things. Was she right that I had to decide what I was willing to work for? I already suspected that careers and travel opportunities weren't served up on buffet platters. The real question was: was I willing to work for a writing career? Was I willing to make time to write *and* be willing to revise, revise, revise (Mr. Pollen's three Rs)? Was I willing to accept my father's compliments about my writing *and* accept other people's criticisms? Was I willing to slave over grammar *and* consider Kerry's suggestion that I stop hiding behind two-dimensional characters and faulty plot lines and live a little? And if I shouted an emphatic "NO!" to those questions, if I chose a different/easier career path and then found out I was dying of cancer, would I regret not making a better go at writing?

"Your arms are getting muscular," Grams said suddenly, derailing my dark thoughts. "You've also lost some weight."

If Grams' rusty old manual scale could be trusted, I'd lost eight pounds. It wasn't like the old lady was starving me, or making me paint for twelve hours at a stretch, but I was getting more exercise than I'd ever had before and Grams didn't stock what she called "empty calories" in the house. Thanks to the sunshine and fresh air, I'd even lost my couch-potato pallor. I felt healthy—physically anyway. I still had a ways to go before I could claim I felt sane about Mike and Barb, Sam and Elizabeth, my career crisis, and Kerry, but—

Kerry?

And speak of the devil, there he was carrying cases of paper napkins and coffee creamers into the café as Grams and I trudged our way up the wharf.

Please don't let him see me, I silently prayed. I hadn't fully processed last night's bizarre nose-biting episode. I was hoping that with time the strange glow Kerry gave me would just go away. After all, he was arrogant, goofy, damaged, and possibly a little bit dangerous. But he made me feel . . . I don't know . . . *happy?* . . . for the first time in months. Best to take Grams' advice and keep my distance.

Yet there he was, waving and beckoning Grams and me toward the café. "Hey, you," he said to me, then turned to Grams. "Hey, Josie. Coffee's on me."

Jenny shot me an appraising look as I trailed into the café after Kerry and Grams; it was like she was looking to discover something smug or hostile in my expression that might justify her cold attitude towards me. I wouldn't give her the satisfaction. I smiled at her instead.

Kerry went behind the counter and poured three cups of coffee. "Milk and sugar?" he asked me.

"Just milk, thanks," I mumbled.

He carried the drinks to a small table and gestured for Grams and I to sit. Straddling a chair backwards, he began telling us about a lake trout he'd caught earlier that morning. Grams was suitably impressed. I didn't know a lake trout from a goldfish, so I kept quiet.

"Kerry, don't you have an appointment in Wawa this morning?" Jenny called from the counter where she was arranging muffins in a display case.

"Not until eleven, Mom!" he called over his shoulder, then poked me under the table with his foot.

I was trying with all my might to avoid direct eye contact with Kerry who was sitting to my right trying with all *his* might to catch my attention, first by staring at me, then by *aheming*, now by poking me under the table with his foot. Each time I shifted my gaze his way, Kerry would grin at me and rub his nose. Every time he did this, I looked up, down, around, desperately wanting to just slide under the table and never come out. I guzzled my coffee. My throat burned. Pain I could handle. Embarrassment was unbearable.

"Kerry," Grams asked, peering at him with concern. "What's wrong with your face?"

"My face?" Mr. Innocent replied.

"You keep rubbing at it."

Kerry kicked me again. "I dreamed last night that someone bit my nose."

"Looks okay to me," Grams observed. If there had been any little residual tooth marks on Kerry's nose, I'd have dropped dead of humiliation right then and there.

Kerry coughed back a laugh. "It wasn't a hard bite, like the way you'd chomp into a crisp apple," he described. "It was more of a gentle, almost tentative bite, like the way you'd nibble at a freshly roasted marshmallow."

That did it.

"Something funny, Charlie-girl?" Kerry winked at me as Grams bent down to grab a napkin that had drifted off the table.

"You should see a therapist about those dreams of yours," I said.

"Yeah. I wonder what Dr. Freud would have to say about the whole thing."

"Well," Grams said, straightening. "I hate to break up such scintillating conversation, but—"

"—we really must get to the post office," I added, eager to make an escape.

"Just let me run to the washroom," Grams said, and disappeared into the back room.

Kerry and I were alone. Even Jenny had retreated into the kitchen to check on her latest batch of muffins. I hoped Kerry would get up, too, but he just kept sitting there at the table grinning at me like a hyena (I'd never actually seen a hyena, grinning or otherwise, but I could imagine it was *not* a pretty sight).

Ignoring him, I hopped up and quickly cleared the table. I took our empty mugs to the counter, then pretended to examine a display of Lake Ringrose postcards.

Kerry snuck up behind me and tapped me on the shoulder. He might as well have shot me with a Taser; I jumped at least three feet.

"Scaredy cat," Kerry snickered. "You can't avoid me forever."

"Just you watch."

"You don't need to be embarrassed," Kerry said, his eyes full of mischief.

What was taking Grams so long? "I'm not embarrassed."

"Besides, you biting my nose wasn't embarrassing. It was a turn-on."

My face burned. "I guess I'm not supposed to be *embarrassed* by that comment, either?"

Kerry laughed. "I wasn't being suggestive, just factual."

"Right."

"But just so you know, I'm attracted to you, too." He thought he had me all figured out. I'd show him. "I'm just being honest," he added.

Jenny returned from the back room, carrying a tray of cheese croissants. "Honest about what?"

Kerry grinned. "Honest when I told Charlie that your home-baked blueberry pies are award-winning, the best in Northern Ontario nine years running." I knew he was being sarcastic; Kerry told me the previous night that Jenny's baked goods were made from mixes.

Jenny scowled. "You'd best be on your way to Wawa, Kerry. I don't want any calls from the police. And I'd like my car back by dinner. Full of gas, please."

"You know, *Mom,*" Kerry said, clearly irritated. "I don't see why I have to go all the way to Wawa to check in with a probation officer. You're clearly up to the task yourself."

Jenny ignored him and turned to me. "So, how are you enjoying Lake Ringrose?"

"Uh, good. Kerry's been showing me around."

Jenny faced her son. "You're behaving yourself, aren't you, Kerry?" she asked.

Kerry laughed. "Haven't you raised me to be a gentleman?"

Jenny sighed. "No one is doubting your charm, Kerry. It's your bad habits that concern me."

A phone rang in the back room. Jenny scurried off to answer it.

Kerry grabbed a set of car keys from the counter and followed Grams and me outside into the clean morning air.

Grams set off with purposeful strides towards the post office, but I hung back. I told myself I didn't want to pry, but my curiosity got the best of me, as usual.

"Kerry," I asked, trailing him towards an old green Corolla. "What did your mother mean by 'your bad habits'?"

He pondered his reply. "I pick my nose? Fart in church? Forget to wash my hands before dinner?"

"And *that's* why you're checking in with a probation officer?"

Kerry looked me square in the eye and gave my shoulder a friendly punch. "Don't worry about my bad habits, Charlie-girl. My bad boy days are over."

I couldn't tell if he thought that was a good or bad thing.

Chapter Fifteen

Gripping the thin blue envelope with exotic Australian postage like a winning lottery ticket, I felt a sharp stab of guilt to my solar plexus for not dropping Sam a line the way Mike had suggested. I played it cool all the way back to Grams' house, but the moment I was alone in Geri's room, I ripped open the envelope.

> *G'day Charlie!*
>
> *I hadn't heard from you in so long, I called Springdale to see if you were still alive. Your dad told me that you were spending the summer up north with your Grams. Remember the Thanksgiving when we were eleven and she beat the pants off us playing basketball in my driveway? I'm taller now, but I'm sure she could still whip my butt.*
>
> *Mike was surprised when I told him you hadn't been writing. Are you mad at me for some reason? Do you have a boyfriend now? Is that why you stopped e-mailing me? We can still be friends, can't we?*
>
> *Since I don't go to school here, I haven't met a lot of kids, except for my girlfriend Elizabeth. She's nineteen and has silky yellow hair—like Aunt Carol's golden retriever. Liz doesn't know I'm only*

sixteen (apparently very tall+very smart=passing for older). We haven't made out or anything, but maybe she's just shy. I know what you're thinking, Charlie. But only a cynic like you would say that she just likes me so I'll help with her computer assignments. Besides, it's not like I want to marry her. I don't even like her that much. But she asked me out, so I figure I might as well see what happens. I'm starting to think that Madame Dumas may not be the most feasible love interest.

Which brings me to something I've been wondering about since you stopped returning my e-mails. You said something to me the night before I left for Australia. I thought you were joking, but maybe you weren't. Do you remember what I'm talking about? I haven't decided which is scarier: that you were serious, or that you weren't.

Write back soon. Please. With nuts and sprinkles on top (I remember that you don't like cherries.)
Sam.

P.S. I haven't written snail mail since I sent that ten-page letter to Pamela Anderson back in fifth grade. Do you think she ever got it?

I looked up from the letter and the world hadn't blown apart the way it might have a few weeks ago, even though Sam had confirmed the worst, that Elizabeth was his—*gulp*—girlfriend. Was it because their relationship clearly wasn't the sappy soap opera romance that I'd envisioned? Or was it simply because my own attention was . . . shifting? Things were so much simpler when Sam and I were in kindergarten and life was about trading Legos and sharing grape popsicles.

Besides Sam's letter, I'd received a postcard from Barb. *The Eaton Center* was printed in glittery script across the top of a glossy four by six depiction of shopping mall mayhem. *Can you spot me?* Barb wrote on the back, trying to be cute. I felt sad for her, almost. She tried so hard to win me over. Hadn't she realized yet I wasn't much of a prize?

Finally, there was a big yellow envelope from Mike. It contained an already-pawed-over copy of a recent *Pulse* and my report card. An oversized sticky note was affixed.

> *Congrats on the A in Creative Writing, but what are we going to do about your other courses? I'm a little surprised that nearly every one of your marks has dropped since last semester. You know you can come to me if you're having trouble in math. Don't get me wrong, Char—I'm not upset with you. Bs aren't bad. But you can't let your marks slip too much if you want to get into your first choice university next year . . .*

I didn't finish the note. Instead, I dialed Mike's cell phone. It was noon; he'd be on his lunch break.

He picked up. I cut quickly to the chase. "Why did I get an *A* in Creative Writing?"

"Uh . . . why not?"

"Mr. Pollen said that unless I revised my final assignment, I'd get a C-minus."

"I guess he changed his mind."

"He had a *heart attack,* Mike! Even if I *had* revised my assignment, which I *didn't,* he wouldn't have had the opportunity to read it. The A must have been a typo," I mused.

"Why in the world would Hector have given you a C-minus?"

"My final assignment lacked plot and character development," I droned.

"I've read some of your stories. You have excellent spelling and use lots of adjectives. Surely that's worth more than a C-minus?"

"What if my assignment was *so bad* it gave him a heart attack, Mike? What if my literary ineptitude *killed* him?"

Mike laughed. "Hector's going to be fine, Char. He's home now."

Relief washed over me like warm bath water. "He's okay?"

"Read the *Cards of Thanks* section in the *Pulse* that I sent you. I've been getting the paper forwarded to me in Toronto."

Promising to call Mike again in a few days, I hung up and quickly rifled through the paper to the Classifieds. Births. Deaths. Help Wanted. For Sale. There it was—*Cards of Thanks*.

> *My deepest gratitude to Dr. Moosehead and the love-ly and competent nurses at the cardiac clinic. Thanks also to those who sent cards and flowers and their best wishes for my speedy recovery. Kudos to the fine neighbors who cut my grass and took excellent care of my sweet dog Hamlet and . . .*

Just like Mr. Pollen to make a note of gratitude sound like a bloody Oscar acceptance speech.

I flipped back to the front of the paper. It was dated July third, more than a week ago.

Did I dare?

I called 411, then Mr. Pollen's home number. My stomach did triple flips as I heard one ring, then two, then three. Just hang up, Charlie; Grams' phone bill will be through the roof.

"Hello?" Mr. Pollen sounded a little winded. What if I'd made him run for the phone from the bathroom or his side porch? What if I gave him another heart attack?

"Mr. Pollen?" I asked. Stupid. Who else would it be?

"Charles? Is that you?"

"Sir, why do you call me Charles?"

"I once had a goldfish named Charles."

"I am *not* teacher's pet material."

"That's for sure."

I let the name thing go. "How are you, Mr. Pollen?"

"Right as rain. Thanks for the lovely hibiscus. I would have thought you'd send a cactus."

I let that go, too. "Sir, was it a typo?"

"Was *what* a typo?"

"My creative writing mark. My report card says I got an A"

"Alas, no."

Had he just been playing head games with me? "But you told me I'd get a C-minus."

Mr. Pollen let out a raspy breath. "After you left my office that last day, I rethought your piece and—"

"You liked it after all?" I grinned into the telephone mouthpiece. Maybe I could really do it, be a writer.

"No!" Mr. Pollen said, bursting my bubble before it had time to inflate to capacity. "But I realized I'd been marking you against what I perceived as your potential instead of against the syllabus. Your writing last semester, though far beneath your abilities, is still superior to that of the others in the class. I realize it's not fair of me to push you to the limit if writing's not something you want to pursue seriously."

Oh.

Mr. Pollen sighed. "Look, I know that my expressions of criticism are frank—some might say harsh. But . . . look, may I be honest with you?"

"Okay." Had he ever been anything but?

"This is what I tell the students in my adult writing class," he said, then coughed. "But I think it's in your best interest to hear it from me now, not when you're thirty-five." Did he really think I was mature enough now to hear whatever "it" was, or did he already know that he wouldn't be around to talk with me about "it"—or anything else—when I was thirty-five?

"I'm listening."

"Fiction writing is a fiercely competitive business. Publishing houses don't coddle new writers; either you have it or you don't. And if you have it—as I believe you do—either you use it and nourish it and grow it . . . or you don't."

"But—"

"No excuses. Look at your friend, Sam. He's tall and can shoot baskets. But despite countless tryouts he can't make the basketball team. Why? Because he spends his free time in cyberspace instead of getting outside and practicing the dribbles and turns and offensive moves that would make him a great player. It's not enough that he has a great free throw. Similarly, it's not enough that *you* have a natural style and a witty way with words. If you want to play the writing game, you have to practice everything, not just what you do well. 'Funny' just isn't enough to get you published."

Mr. Pollen waited for me to say something, but his sermon had rendered me speechless. "Well, Charlena," he said after ten seconds passed and I was still gaping into the mouthpiece. "Have a nice summer."

"Mr. Pollen?" I croaked.

"Yes?"

"I'm glad you're feeling like your old self again."

He chuckled. "Thank you, Charlena."

"And Mr. Pollen?"

"Mmmm?" He waited.

"Don't give up on me, sir."

"Don't give up on yourself."

It was Mr. Pollen's voice on the phone, but it was my mother's sketchbook talking. That was its message.

The *first* message.

> *Hey Sam!*
>
> *I'm sorry for not writing sooner. Back in Springdale I was busy with exams and now, at Lake Ringrose, I'm busy painting walls and canoeing to the village on errands. (Grams rarely uses her car, which she proudly admits was purchased the same year Elvis died!)*
>
> *Everyone here at Lake Ringrose tells me how much I look like my mother. People even do double takes when they see me, like they've seen a ghost. And I keep getting a creepy feeling that they all know something I don't know.*
>
> *On a lighter note:*
>
> *a) A married couple at the lake have shingled their entire cottage with aluminum pop cans. Is it "recycling" or just "ri-diculous?"*

b) There's an eighty-five year old lady who sunbathes naked on her dock every morning; is there an age cap on your attraction to older women?

c) I discovered I was named after my mother's pet chipmunk. A chipmunk! Should I be grateful it wasn't a skunk?

d) There's a guy here, Kerry, who lives in a tree house and plays guitar. He let me drive his ATV yesterday and I helped him dig worms to sell to the marina. His mother's a psycho-bitch who treats me like I've got rabies or worse, but Kerry is fun to be with. We goof around, the way you and I used to once upon a time.

Of course I remember what I said to you the night before you left for Australia. I'd throw myself in front of a bus for you, Sam. Give you a kidney. Slay a dragon. But there are different kinds of love. Far be it from me to dissuade you from dating Elizabeth with the golden retriever hair. Best of luck to you, mate!

Eat a vegemite sandwich for me,
Charlie

Chapter Sixteen

For almost a week it rained—a cold, blustery rain that kept Grams and I holed up in the house painting her kitchen in the mornings and sitting by the fireplace working jigsaws or playing Monopoly through the afternoons.

One rainy night, Jenny Sanderson materialized on the doorstep. Grams made a pot of tea and steered Jenny into the den. Sensing I wasn't welcome at their powwow, I announced that I was going to take a shower. As I undressed and inspected my fading tan lines, snippets of conversation could be heard through the bathroom's air vents.

"I don't think we need to worry, Jenny," Grams said.

Worry? Worry about what?

Then a few seconds later, " . . . she doesn't make friends easily . . . you said yourself Kerry's been easier to live with . . . it's good for him to have another teenager to talk to . . . Charlena won't steer him down the wrong paths . . . maybe it's even time for the truth to—"

"No!" Jenny shouted.

"Shhh!" Grams replied.

I pressed my ear over the vent. The voices were lower now, almost whispers.

" . . . It's been a bad situation from the start . . ."

" . . . too many secrets . . ."

" . . . she'd be devastated if . . ."

" . . . Kerry is just like his . . ."

" . . . maybe it's you, Jenny, that can't . . ."

I shifted my weight. The floor creaked. The voices stopped suddenly, then began again, just murmurs now, indecipherable.

I stepped into the shower and turned the taps on full blast. But nothing could wash away my confusion.

The rain gave way to a blistering heat wave that finally got me swimming in the lake. When I wasn't attacked by swarms of goldfish or swallowed up by a monster my first few times out, I relaxed and started doing laps to and from the floating dock twenty meters from shore. My arms and shoulders were stronger now from frequent canoeing and the ceaseless back and forth of the paint rollers. I sometimes found myself swimming for over an hour at a stretch.

One morning I pulled myself out of the water at Grams' dock, stretched out flat on my back in the sunrise, and let myself be lulled by the warm breeze. I wondered if I'd be able to remember these occasional moments of peace, feel the sense of calm that sometimes took me by surprise, once I returned to Springdale.

In the past, I'd relied on my memory to recount events and feelings about things. But just being away from the familiarity of home for the first time, I was learning how quickly memories of places and events and feelings—even people's faces—became distorted and diluted by time. The night I'd gone with Kerry to the tree house, I'd written about the adventure in my ghastly, furry puppy journal. Since then, I'd had a strange compulsion to continue writing every night before bed. But I didn't know if my writing could ever accurately describe the wow-factor of the Lake Ringrose sunrise, or the jelly in my knees every time Kerry laughed at one of my stupid quips. Mr. Pollen always said that by keeping a journal, I could go back weeks, months, even *years* and recapture ideas and feelings, then use them to direct my writing—and my life. Was it really true that ten or twenty years from now I could gather the scribbles of the past few days and use them to fuel a novel?

It could go either way.

I closed my eyes and concentrated on the moist pine breeze tickling my skin. Days like this, I shouldn't be worrying about the future. I should be focusing on the here and now, the serenity. *Carpe diem* and all that shit.

"AHHHHHHHHHHHH!" I screamed. There was something slithering across my stomach.

A stifled guffaw.

"Get it off! GET IT OFF NOW!"

More snickering.

I jumped up, grabbed the snake, flung it onto the rocky shore, and let out a string of profanity.

"Hey, you." Kerry was keeled over at the end of the dock, clutching his ribs, shaking with laughter.

"Why the hell did you put that thing on me!"

"It's just a baby garter snake."

"Asshole!" I got up and pushed Kerry hard, hard enough that he lost his balance and fell off the dock into the water. He came up choking on water, still in stitches. He reached up, grabbed my left ankle, and pulled me into the water after him. We went a full round spraying and dunking each other.

"Everything okay down there?" Grams appeared at the top of the steps. Doc Will was at her side, carrying a clipboard.

Kerry waved cheerfully. "Hey, Josie, Will. Did you hear that potty-mouth Charlie-girl cussing me out?"

"I imagine the whole lake did."

"He put a snake on me!" I protested.

Kerry laughed. "Tattletale."

Grams frowned. "You're not working today, Kerry?"

He pointed to the Kendriks', three houses away. A new dock was in pieces on the shore. "Just taking a break."

Doc Will marched down to join Kerry and me on the dock. He tapped a pen against his clipboard. "I'm in charge of the Labour Day Weekend Committee this summer. How would the two of you feel about partnering up for the Four Islands Race? I'm looking to get at least ten teams signed up this morning."

Kerry grinned. "Great idea!"

"What's the Four Islands Race?" In my experience, "race" meant some sort of competitive sporting event. Not my style.

"There's a big festival in the village on Labour Day weekend each year," Kerry explained. "It kicks off Saturday with the Four Islands Race. Teams of two race in canoes across the lake and back. There are pit stops at four designated islands where extra challenges are set up: obstacle courses, scavenger hunts, relay races, whatever. The team that arrives back at the village dock with the best time wins a basket of free stuff from local businesses."

"I don't know what gave you the impression I was an athlete."

Kerry reached over and squeezed my left bicep. "Almost as big as mine."

Right. "Wouldn't someone else in the village be a better partner for you?" I asked. "Someone who knows the trail? I'll probably wreck your chances of winning the championship."

Kerry shook his head. "The village council changes the trail and the challenges every year, right, Will? That's part of the fun; no one knows what to expect. I raced with Lisa last summer, but she won't be here this year—or ever again, if she can help it. The teams have to be male-female, aged sixteen or older."

"Mike will be coming to take me home that weekend," I said.

Doc Will beamed. "Great! You can show him all your fancy canoe moves."

"I don't know if I can keep up with you," I told Kerry. "I can paddle and swim, but I'm not much of a runner, or—"

Kerry laughed. "You're talking to a guy with screws in both femurs and an artificial kneecap; I can run faster on my hands. I just want to do the race for fun. I don't care if we win. Joe and Lily, two summer cottagers from Thunder Bay, have taken first prize three years running. But it's still early summer; we could train together, give them a run for their money. How about it?"

"I've got to be on my way into town, Charlena," Doc Will said. "Can I put your name down?"

Hmm. Kerry and I could train. Together. "Oh, okay," I said.

"That's the spirit!" Doc will thumped me on the back enthusiastically. "We'll make a Lake Ringrose girl out of you yet!"

"I've got to be going, too," Kerry said after Doc Will said his goodbyes. "Maybe we can get together tomorrow to plan our training strategy? After dinner? I'm making another bait run to the pond; we can talk along the way."

"Okay."

Kerry waved to Grams, winked at me, and waded his way back along the shore to the Kendriks', whistling the theme song from *Gilligan's Island*.

"Kerry's legs must really hurt sometimes," I said, joining Grams at the top of the stairs.

She nodded. "I imagine a lot of him hurts sometimes. Ready for lunch?"

Over grilled cheese on whole wheat and sliced cantaloupe, Grams elaborated on the Four Islands Race and offered to let Kerry and me use her canoe. "But remember what I said about Kerry, Charlena. Have fun, but be careful is all."

I groaned. "Grams, I *told* you, I'm not looking for a summer fling."

"Sometimes flings find you whether you go looking for them or not."

I puffed out my cheeks with exasperation. "Grams, nothing *sexual* is going on with Kerry and me if that's what you're worried about. And so what if it was? I'm not eleven years old anymore."

"Kerry is not what he seems."

"I know he's on probation. Is it that?"

Grams shook her head.

"Then what?"

"Charlena, you've just got to trust me on this. Don't get mixed up with him."

"Has he got hepatitis or AIDS or something?"

"No. Look, I just don't want to see you get hurt. Either of you."

Ludicrous. "You think *I'd* hurt Kerry?"

Grams shrugged. "He's gone through *terrible* times this year. His father died tragically. He was seriously injured and spent many months in rehab. He has to re-do his senior year if he wants his high school diploma. *And* he's got those damn drug charges on his record."

"*Drugs?*"

"You said you knew."

"I said I knew he was on probation. Kerry didn't say why."

Grams sighed. "Well, now you know."

"Is he an addict? A trafficker?"

Grams frowned. "It's not my place to discuss it. Suffice to say, if Kerry were either of those things, I wouldn't let you near him, let alone allow you to go off into the woods with him."

"Then I don't understand."

"Charlena, I'm sorry, but I cannot—*will not*—discuss it with you. I encourage you and Kerry to be friends, but you must remain *just* friends."

I couldn't drop it. "You know, Grams, you claim Kerry is so troubled, but he sure seems pretty well-adjusted to me."

"*Seems* is right. He's hanging by a thread. I've known Kerry since the day he was born and though he's had a long string of bikini-clad girlfriends and party buddies over the years, I don't think he's ever had any real friends, except maybe his sister Lisa, but she's gone now, too. Be someone special to him, Charlena; it would do him a world of good to have a real friend to spend time with. Talk to him. Train for the race with him. Just don't be another notch on his pine tree or however that saying goes. You both deserve better. Promise me."

"Okay, Grams. I promise," I agreed, but who was I kidding? How was I supposed to turn off what Kerry's crazy antics, infuriating comments, and those Brad Pitt lips did to my insides? And did I even want to?

It *seemed* that Grams had developed a bad case of unnecessary over-protectiveness.

Chapter Seventeen

After supper the next evening, I answered a rap on Grams'
kitchen door and found Kerry gesturing to two old mountain
bikes propped against a tree.

"Hey, you. Feel like cycling to the pond tonight? Mom hid
the keys to the ATV."

"Why?"

"I told her you and I were partnering up for the Four
Islands Race—just trying to make civilized conversation—
and she went *apeshit.* Told me I was spending too much time
with you. Said I should be spending my leisure hours doing
physiotherapy and studying last year's school books. I should
not, in her words, be *gallivanting* with you."

"Does your mother think I have fleas, or the Ebola virus,
or what?"

Kerry laughed. "Ah, don't take it personally. She's just terrified I'll turn into my father unless she stops me from having any fun for the rest of my life."

Grams emerged from the den, her celebrity crossword
book in tow. "I thought I heard your voice, Kerry."

"Hey, Babe," he said, planting a kiss on her cheek. Grams
giggled and swatted him away. What the hell? Why was it
okay for Kerry to flirt with Grams but not with me? Let's be

serious, it couldn't have been because she wanted him for herself. (I'm all for older women dating younger guys, but Grams was *forty-four years* older than Kerry; that's just gross.)

"I must be going deaf, Kerry," she said. "Usually I hear you coming a mile away."

"Cruella nabbed my keys again."

Grams laid a hand on his arm. "Don't be too hard on Jenny, Kerry; she's still your mother. After all that's happened this year, she can't help but wish you'd stick closer to home."

Kerry gave Grams a hard stare. "Josie, that's a lie and you know it. You don't have a problem with me spending time with Charlie, do you?"

She stared back. "It depends how the two of you are spending your time."

Kerry sighed. "Josie, Josie. You know I'm saving myself for you."

Grams sighed, too, and waved us off. "Not too late, okay?"

"We'll try to make it back by nightfall; Charlie-girl doesn't like the bats."

"Bullshit," I mumbled.

"No, *guano,*" Grams replied.

"What?"

"Batshit; it's called *guano.*"

Grams and Kerry cracked up.

We pedaled slowly to the pond. Kerry was unusually quiet. Something was bothering him besides his rickety knees on the inclines.

We leaned the bikes against a stump, made fast work of collecting the worms and minnows, then climbed up into the tree house to escape the mosquitoes. Kerry opened his food cache, tossed me a Coke, and took one for himself. We plunked down on the plank floor, our backs against the wall, and stretched out our legs.

"You look like you'd rather have a beer," I said, trying for a little levity.

Kerry took a long swig of Coke and stifled a burp. "I don't drink. Not anymore."

"Me, either," I said.

Kerry raised an eyebrow at me.

"Okay, I never did, really. Well, maybe a few beers at the odd party."

"You ever smoked?" Kerry asked.

I nodded. "When Sam and I were nine, we found a pack of Belmont Milds behind the bleachers in the school yard. We smoked about five each, then threw up all over each other."

"You ever smoked weed?"

"Yeah. Once. During the sophomore band trip to Montreal. There was a party at my billet's house and—"

Kerry laughed. "*You* were in the school band?"

"Flute. I'm not musical; I just like the trips."

"Hmm." Kerry said.

"What?"

"Maybe I'll tell you later. Sorry to interrupt. There was a party and . . . ?"

"No big deal. Some kids passed around a joint. I was too terrified of getting caught to feel much of a buzz. End of story. Sorry to disappoint you; I've never been much of a wild child."

"It's not what it's cracked up to be."

"Not if you end up with drug charges," I said. Kerry eyed me with curiosity. "Sorry," I added. "Grams let it slip."

He shrugged. "It's not a secret. And I wasn't just charged; I was convicted. Cocaine possession. Guilty as charged." He paused a long time. "But just so you don't get the wrong impression, the drugs weren't mine."

Right.

"They were my dad's."

Sure, blame it on a dead guy. "Then why are you taking the rap?" I asked. And why did Kerry's father *have* drugs? I knew *kids* who did drugs, but their *parents?*

Kerry flicked a spider off his shoulder. "I got off easy, Charlie-girl. I had enough cocaine on me to be sent to the pen for ten years. Three years probation is a slap on the wrist."

"But—"

"We're supposed to be working out a training schedule for the Four Islands Race, not talking about me." He took a long swig of Coke.

"I don't mean to pry. It's just—"

Kerry shook his head. "It's not that I think you're nosy; in fact, I'd rather *everyone* just asked me what happened last New Year's Eve instead of gossiping behind my back. But I don't want to bring you down with the grim details of my life. *The Young And The Restless* has nothing on the Sandersons."

"I don't mind."

Kerry didn't reply. He lay down on the tree house floor and started doing sit-ups. After about two hundred he stopped and sat up, wiped sweat off his forehead with the back of his hand. "Today would have been my father's forty-first birthday. Lisa never called. Mom never even let on she remembered."

Holy cow. Every year, even now, Mike and I went to visit Geri's grave on her birthday. I wouldn't forget her birthday any sooner than I'd forget my own.

"I don't know what's wrong with me today," Kerry continued. "I've been feeling okay about things lately. I even invited you here today to talk about the race so I wouldn't have to mope around alone tonight thinking about Dad. But I'm doing it anyway. We'd better just go." Kerry stood up fast and bumped his head hard on a ceiling beam. He cursed, then motioned for me to get up, too. He chewed his lip the way I did when I forced myself not to cry.

I patted the spot of floor beside me, "Let's not go just yet. Finish your drink."

Kerry sighed and plunked back down. We sat quietly awhile with our backs against the wall. Kerry kicked off his Tevas and wiggled his toes.

"You know," I said, "I read somewhere that people whose second toes are longer than their big toes have higher IQs than the general population."

Kerry frowned. "Tell that to Mr. Beaufort down at the community school."

I tried for a save. "Or maybe it was higher sex drive."

Finally, a laugh. "Let me see *your* toes," Kerry demanded.

"No way!"

Kerry made a play for my ankles and had my sneakers and socks off before I could put up a fight. He wrinkled up his nose. "Phhew."

"My feet do not stink!" I protested.

"Then that sudden stench must be a dead squirrel." He ducked my effort to whack him across the head. "Hmm," he remarked, holding my ankle and observing my foot like it were a science project. "Your second toe is longer, too."

"Have you ever noticed Grams' feet?" I asked. "Her toenails are yellow and bulging with fungus. Totally revolting."

Trist

133

"Are your feet ticklish?" Kerry asked.

"No."

"Liar." Kerry lunged for my feet again.

"Stop! Stop! I have to pee." I really did have to pee. "Kerry, where's the ladies' room?"

"We're in the middle of a forest; do like the bears do."

I crawled over to the floor hatch. "Easy for you to say."

"Here." Kerry tossed me a roll of toilet paper from one of his supply boxes. "Don't squat on any poison ivy."

When I came back to the tree house a few minutes later, Kerry had stretched out on the air bed. "Hey, you," he said, looking miserable again. I made him scootch over and stretched out beside him.

"Kerry?" I said.

He rolled onto his back and stared up at the roof beams. "Yeah?"

"Want to hear a story?"

He didn't reply, so I told him one anyway.

"One of the very few memories I have of my mother is of Halloween a few months before she died. I sat with her on the porch when the older kids from the neighborhood came around trick-or-treating. She let me give out the candy. I thought that was the real treat, getting to be the helper. She wore a rainbow-colored clown wig. It must have been to cover her head—she was bald from chemo—but to me she looked just beautiful. I think about her every time I see a clown."

I'd never told anyone about that memory before. Not Mike, not Sam, not Grams. No one had ever asked about the tiny clown key chain that dangled from my school knapsack. I wasn't quite sure why I was telling Kerry now; it just felt right.

Except that tear was snaking its way from the corner of Kerry's left eye over his temple towards his ear. Oh, my God. I didn't mean to make him cry. I'd never *seen* a teenage guy cry before. I didn't even know eighteen-year-old guys *could* cry. What the hell was I supposed to do now?

"Kerry?" I asked. "What happened with you and your dad?"

Chapter Eighteen

"My father was a forty-year-old party boy," Kerry started. "He let me drink beer with him on fishing trips since I was ten. Rented porno movies for my thirteenth birthday party. Supplied me with condoms before I ever had a girlfriend. I used to play softball in Wawa. After every win, he'd take me and my teammates out behind the bleachers and share a joint with us. He let me do whatever I wanted: loud parties in the village, co-ed ski trips, underage outings to strip bars."

"When did your father get involved in cocaine? I mean, weed is one thing, but *cocaine?*" The thought of Mike involved in some seedy drug underworld almost made me laugh out loud.

Kerry shook his head. "I don't know anything. Not when, how, or even *why* Dad got involved in cocaine. But last fall I knew he'd been up to *something*. He was hyper and irritable all the time. He looked haggard. He'd be scheduled to arrive home from a haul on Saturday night and not show up until Monday morning. Mom assumed he was having another affair on the road. *I* wondered if he'd started gambling or something. But I don't think *anyone* suspected that he was running cocaine all over Northern Ontario."

"You ever tried it?" I asked.

"Cocaine? Nah. I don't even know if my father ever did it. All I know is that New Year's Eve he had a mother lode of it on him and he knew that the cops were closing in."

My brain was spinning back in time. What was I doing last New Year's Eve? Watching the latest Harry Potter movie on DVD. Eating Cheetos. Bored because Sam was visiting relatives. Pissed off because Mike was spending the evening with Barb instead of me. Seemed tragic at the time. Seemed tame and stupid now.

Kerry rolled off the air mattress and took his time replenishing our drinks. He wandered back, lay down, sat back up again, fiddled with the drawstring on his hooded sweatshirt. Stalling.

"Dad dropped me off in his pickup at the annual party at the village hall around seven. He was going into Wawa to see a guy about getting some emergency repairs done on his rig—he kept it there in a trucker's lot behind the gas station. He said he'd be back around midnight."

"Where was your mother?"

"She went early to the village hall to drop off some refreshments, then drove right back home. Other years she's stayed to do full-scale catering and cleanup, but Lisa took off back to school that morning instead of sticking around to help her out like she usually did."

"Lisa hates Lake Ringrose so much she'd miss the New Year's party?"

Kerry snorted. "If Lisa and I didn't look so much alike, I'd swear she was adopted. Her only goal since kindergarten has been to *get out* of Lake Ringrose. Escape the fucked-up family fold. I can't really blame her. Dad was always drinking and carrying on. And as I'm sure you've noticed, Mom would rather raise pit bulls than children. And I'm stupid, so—"

"You aren't *stupid!*"

"Compared to Lisa, I'm about three brain cells away from useless."

"Then stop comparing yourself to Lisa."

"Easy for you to say," Kerry replied.

"Right." I had no one to compare myself to. Certainly not Sam with his techno smarts and travel opportunities. Or Aussie Elizabeth with her golden retriever hair. Or Barb with her boundless energy and chronic cheerfulness.

Kerry wiped his nose on his wrist. "You want to hear the rest of this story or not?"

"Yeah, I do. Please, go on."

"The New Year's party at the village hall is the same every year," Kerry continued. "Until midnight, all the families eat, dance, and socialize. Then, after the 'Happy New Year!' hoopla, the teenagers pair off behind the stage curtains, the women take the little kids home, and the men pull out cards and drink until they pass out on the pool table."

I smirked. "So I guess you were behind the curtains with some lucky girl that night?"

"No such luck. My girlfriend—that Wawa girl I told you about—was visiting relatives up in Marathon. I figured I'd just hang out with my poker buddies until Dad showed up, drink a few beers with him, then head home while we could still tie our own boots. You want a granola bar?"

I shook my head. How could he think of food at a time like this? "What happened when your dad showed up? *Did* he show up?"

"Yeah, but it was late, almost one a.m. Dad rushed over to where I was dealing another round and told me we had to leave—right away. If I hadn't been drinking so much, I might have thought it weird that he kept peering over his shoulder out the window, like he was waiting for someone to come."

"And it was too late in the season for Santa Claus," I hazarded a guess.

"Exactly. So while I was getting my coat, Dad stuffed a big, wrapped package into the cargo pocket of my pants. He told me it was some of Mrs. Larkin's homemade sausage. We were always getting stuff like that from the neighbors; it wouldn't have triggered a warning bell even if I'd been stone cold sober. Heading out, I asked Dad about the rig repairs. He said that everything had been taken care of, and that he wanted to get home quickly to rest up for a long haul in the morning. Now *that* should have tipped me off, because the next day was Sunday, not to mention New Year's Day; his company never sent trucks out on weekends or holidays."

I was such a baby, giving Mike the silent treatment for days after he left me alone last New Year's. But what had been so bad about him taking his girlfriend out for dinner and a movie? (He'd even invited me to join them, but I refused.) At least he wasn't sneaking around with drugs or sausages or whatever Kerry was trying to tell me Greg was doing.

Kerry cracked his knuckles. "Outside, Dad whispered that he had a surprise for me, a belated Christmas present he'd brought home from Wawa in the bed of his pickup. He led me around the back of the hall. There in the snow was a GLX4. Brand new. Dad said he'd parked the pickup at home and drove the GLX4 into the village for a test drive."

"What's a GLX4?"

"A snowmobile. The *Rolls Royce* of snowmobiles. No way my father, with his trucker's pay, could have afforded it; he'd just paid Lisa's university costs for the year. That should have

frost

tipped me off, too. How had Dad suddenly come up with so much cash for Lisa's school *and* a brand new snowmobile for me when a year ago he'd bitch for days if one of us asked him for fifty bucks to buy a pair of jeans? But I just stood there like an idiot, sputtering thanks while Dad's eyes kept darting up the road. He tossed me the keys and told me we'd better haul ass home, get the sausages into the freezer."

Kerry paused and began chewing at his lip again. He was getting to the bad part, I could tell. My heart pounded, anxious to hear more about the snowmobile accident Grams had told me about, but not sure if I could handle hearing it from Kerry, who was obviously in so much pain. You asked for this, I scolded myself.

"Charlie-girl, I'm no boy scout, but drunk driving has never been my style. I handed Dad back the keys and asked him to take us home. I didn't want to run my gift into a snowbank." His voice broke. "Christ, giving Dad back the keys that night was the stupidest goddamn thing I've ever done. If I hadn't been trying to act responsibly the old man would still be alive. He'd be in *jail,* but he'd be alive."

It was a hot, dry evening, but Kerry shivered like it was winter again. The hairs on his arms and legs were standing on end. "Dad hopped on the snowmobile and took the controls. I got on behind him. Headlights came around the bend. It could have been anyone—it was just regular headlights—but Dad revved the GLX4 and instead of heading for home, he took off towards the marina like he had a black bear on his ass. When we reached the wharf, he paused just long enough to glance back over his shoulder. Then, without a word of explanation, he fired the snowmobile down the boat launch and out onto the lake."

I noticed my breath was coming out in short gasps, in sync with Kerry's. "But . . . Grams said . . . the lake doesn't freeze over until the end of January."

"Dad knew that, Charlie. He *knew.* I was *screaming* at him to stop. He just went faster."

I shifted my weight on the air mattress and my hand bumped Kerry's hand accidentally. He took it and held it tight. "Whoever had driven into the village followed us to the boat launch. Over my shoulder, I could see headlights glaring out at us. Another car joined the first, red lights rolling, sirens blaring over the roar of the GLX4. *'Dad!'* I pounded on his back. *'It's the OPP! We've got to go back!'* But he flicked off the headlamp and kept racing full speed ahead, not along the shoreline towards our house, but further out, onto the middle of the lake. I tried to figure out what he was thinking. That maybe that we could lose the police and hide out on one of the islands awhile. Or make it across to the old mine and lay low." Kerry let go of my hand and sat up. He crushed his empty Coke can and hurled it hard against the far wall. The tree house shook. "Sorry," he mumbled and hid his face in his hands.

I didn't know what to say, what to do. Should I wrap my arms around him, or try to change the subject, or—

"My father lived at Lake Ringrose all his life," Kerry continued before I could decide. "I guess he lost his bearings in the dark. He didn't see the rock jutting above the ice surface. We hit full speed and went airborne."

Oh my God.

"I broke my legs on that first hit; they took the full impact of the crash. Dad slackened against me . . . died instantly."

I couldn't imagine what Kerry was feeling, but I felt suddenly so sick.

He took a long breath, then spoke in fast, clipped phrases, like if he paused for even a second he might disintegrate. "On the second impact, I was thrown off the snowmobile. About twenty feet onto solid ice. Broke an arm and some ribs. Banged my head up good. Blacked out, I guess. When I came to, I couldn't move. So quiet. I thought for a second that everything was okay. That Dad had got away. Or had gone for help. Then I heard water gurgling a few feet to my right and I knew: the snowmobile—*my* snowmobile—had gone down on a soft spot. Everything went black again." Kerry coughed and gasped for air.

Coke churned in my stomach, threatening to rise and choke me the way Kerry's words were choking him.

"Next thing I remember," Kerry said, "was waking up in a recovery room after emergency surgery. The doctors told me that I'd been rescued by police emergency services and airlifted to Sault Ste. Marie in the Doc's bushplane. God, if it weren't for the fast actions of the police that had come to arrest my dad, I'd have died out there, too. As it were, I was *almost* dead: multiple injuries, severe blood loss, hypothermia, shock. First thing, I asked, 'Where my father? Is he okay?' No one said anything. I knew then for sure. He was dead. That he'd gone down in the lake. That he was gone. *I would have tried to save him if I could.*"

"I know." I reached out with my other hand and squeezed Kerry's arm. It felt like a block of ice. Was he going into shock again?

Kerry took a few deep breaths. Let them out slowly. Fought to keep his voice steady. "Dad's body was . . . found the next day. The OPP recovery crew thought that he might . . . float away under the ice, but they found him at first light. Pinned . . . against the rock. Under open water."

I marveled at how Kerry could be functional enough to tell me all this. If Mike died under similar circumstances, I'd be catatonic. A drooling zombie. For years. That Kerry could get out of bed in the morning at all, not to mention eat and work and crack jokes, amazed me. Maybe it was because he was older. Maybe it was because he was stronger than me in a way that had nothing to do with his biceps.

"I missed the funeral. Lisa said it was horrible, everyone standing around giving each other 'I told you so' glances. There's not much sympathy for people who die in accidents caused by their own reckless habits. Any third grader can tell you that drugs are bad. Lisa says Dad spent his entire life skating on thin ice and it finally got the best of him."

It got *all* of him. "I'm so sorry, Kerry," I said. And I was. It felt so strange. I couldn't remember a time when I'd felt sorry for anyone but myself. And for what? Had anything in my life ever been as bad as what Kerry had been through? Not even close.

"Dad wasn't perfect. He goddamned nearly killed me. And he got me in a hell of a mess getting me to carry that bundle of cocaine for him; it was still in my pants pocket when they cut them off me at the hospital." Kerry chuckled darkly. "The cops planted a guard outside my room—like a guy in a body cast is just going to get up and walk out?"

"Did you ever find out what was going on that night?"

Kerry shook his head. "The cops *still* haven't figured out where the drugs came from, where the *snowmobile* came from, where the drugs were headed, or even who the anonymous caller was that tipped them off to my dad. They filed charges against me, although they knew all along that the drugs weren't mine. To this day, they assume I was somehow involved; they can't imagine how anyone could be stupid enough to think a package of cocaine was *sausages*. Lisa keeps telling me to make peace with the situation and move on, but how do I do that? How can I make peace with what happened if I'll *never know* what really happened? All I got out of this experience was two bum legs, a rap sheet, a year of school down the toilet. I should hate my father, but you know what?"

It was obvious by the catch in Kerry's voice. "You still love him."

"Crazy, or what? My father taught me everything I know about fishing, about rods and live baits and lures, and how to tell a junk fish from a keeper. He never made me feel bad that I wasn't top of my class at school or that I wanted to make a life at Lake Ringrose instead of chase a big-city career like Lisa. He knew that I loved the lake as much as he did, and he was proud of me for it. But look at me now. I'm broken and scarred. I'm eighteen years old and I don't know even who I am anymore," Kerry said.

"You're still you," I said, stupidly, because really, how would I know?

Kerry frowned. "I'm not. Since the accident, just the smell of beer makes me want to puke. I haven't had so much as a drag off a joint. During the summers when my school buddies were away, I used to hang out at the wharf with the wild summer kids, but they can't relate to a guy who doesn't want to party anymore. And my mother's so angry at me all the time. Maybe if I'd gotten jail time she'd be happier. Or maybe she just wishes I'd died instead of Dad." Kerry flopped back down on the air bed and started to sob. "I wish that, too, sometimes." He rubbed angrily at his eyes. "I'm sorry, Charlie-girl. I . . . it's just . . . I miss him."

Without thinking, I turned towards Kerry on the mattress and hugged him. He buried his face in my sweatshirt and cried for what seemed like a half-hour as the evening sun dipped behind the trees.

Branches snapped loudly at the base of the pines. Kerry and I shot apart. He put a finger to his lips and soundlessly rolled off the air bed. Put a swollen eye to a crack in the floorboard, then gestured for me to crouch down beside him. "Check this out. Don't scream. You'll scare them away."

Holding my breath, I put my eye to the crack, blinked hard.

A female moose and her small calf were feasting on branches. Until then, my only moose experience had been made of chocolate. I watched them for a full five minutes, mesmerized, until they wandered out of my sight line into the bush.

Kerry looked a little better. "Hey, you. I'm sorry about all that blubbering." He reached over for the roll of toilet paper, ripped off a few sheets, and blew his nose. "No wonder everyone wants to keep us a safe distance apart; I'm a bloody mess."

"You feel better now?" I asked.

"I feel like I just ran a marathon, but yeah, I guess it was nice to get some of the weight off my chest. It's been so long since anyone's hugged me."

"Anytime, friend."

Kerry cracked open two more Cokes. The Marrotts would have their addition done by Labour Day at the rate Kerry and I were putting away the pops.

"To friends," he said, and we clinked cans.

Chapter Nineteen

For the next thirty minutes, Kerry gave me his take on the Four Islands Race. He explained the previous year's race route, what the challenges were, where he saw our strengths and weaknesses.

"There's a dance afterwards," he added. "Outdoors on the wharf. There's always some crazy theme. Everyone comes. Most of the village kids are back home from camp or their park jobs by then, so it's a big reunion party. And for the summer cottagers, it's time to say goodbye."

"I'm leaving that weekend, too," I reminded him.

Kerry shook his head. "Not until I get a dance."

"I don't dance."

"At all?"

Okay, so I was a freak. They had dances at Springdale High, but Sam and I never went, what with us being semi-social misfits and all.

"Then I'll demonstrate," Kerry exclaimed, struggling to his feet.

That I had to see.

"Fast dancing is easy," he explained. "Just wave your arms and shake your butt in time to the beat. Like this." Kerry boogied around the tree house, wiggling his hips and making funny faces. I cracked up.

Kerry sobered. "I used to be a better dancer."

I raised an eyebrow.

"Okay, maybe not. Anyway, slow dancing requires a partner. So come here. Closer," Kerry said. "We need to be able to touch each other. We did okay on the mattress, didn't we?"

"Yeah." But the mattress had been about comforting a friend in his time of need. Dancing was about . . . *dancing.* I moved a bit closer.

Kerry put his hands on my waist. I flinched a little as happy sparks shot through me. He mistook it as hesitation. "If you aren't comfortable, we can stop."

"No. This is fine," I admitted. Fine. Fantastic. Wow. Whatever.

"You need to find a comfortable place to put your hands," Kerry instructed.

"That's easy." I reached up and wrapped my hands around his throat in a strangle-hold.

"Wrong answer. Try again."

I rested my hands on Kerry's shoulders, hoping he couldn't feel them shaking.

"Much better. Let me put on some music."

Kerry let go of me and extracted a portable radio from his seemingly bottomless box of supplies. He played with the dial and a few seconds later, a sappy, static-filled, slow song filled the tree house.

We took position once again. "Ready?" Kerry asked.

"I'll try not to stomp on your feet."

"Not bad!" Kerry exclaimed when the song ended. The next was an old Bryan Adams ballad. "Want to continue?"

"Okay." Okay? Who was I kidding? This dance thing was making my toes tingle, my heart race like a thoroughbred.

The third song was an upbeat pop tune by a pre-teen boy band. Kerry made a face and switched it off. He walked back towards me and took me so off-guard that I almost fell backwards through the floor hatch. "Can I kiss you, Charlie-girl?"

"You . . . you didn't ask before . . . that . . . that time you kissed my nose," I stammered.

"Ah, that was just about me being goofy," Kerry explained. "This is . . ." He didn't finish the sentence; his lips were otherwise engaged. Over the next few minutes, my inexperienced self developed a whole new respect for what's commonly described in trashy paperback novels as "romantic bliss."

"So," Kerry asked when we broke for air, "was it fireworks for you, too, or just your basic snap, crackle, and pop?"

"*Fireworks?* My amateur lips gave you *fireworks?*"

"You must have natural talent. Or maybe it's the flute playing. According to Lisa—she used to play the clarinet—woodwind players develop stronger and more flexible embouchures than the general population. That makes them better kissers."

"Embou-what?" The word sounded familiar. I knew I should have paid more attention in music class.

"Lip coordination, Charlie-girl. Who's the smarty pants now?" And he kissed me again. And again. And . . .

"Want to move back over to the mattress?" Kerry said into my ear a few minutes later.

Absolutely. I wanted to kiss him forever. Run my hands over his bare chest. Let his fingers—the ones that were perilously close to what my sixth-grade sex-ed teacher called "The Danger Zone"—wander at will. "Probably not a good idea," I said.

Kerry checked his watch. "You're right. It's getting late. I don't want my mother flying out here on her broomstick to chew us out."

It was five minutes before pitch dark when Kerry dropped me to the top of Grams' driveway. "Keep the bike for the rest of the summer," he offered. "Lisa won't miss it."

"Thanks." I didn't know what else to say. How do you talk to a guy who just gave you Real Kiss Number One through Number Fifty Plus?

Kerry looked down the lane towards Grams' house, where the porch lights were burning bright. "So I guess we keep quiet about this, about . . . us?"

I nodded, but made no move to leave.

"Listen, Charlie-girl, I'm taking the bus down to the hospital in Sault Ste. Marie tomorrow. I'll be gone a few days," Kerry said.

"What! Are you okay? Are you sick?"

He laughed. "Relax. It's just a follow-up appointment with my orthopedic surgeon. I'll drop by to see you as soon as I get back. We'll need to start serious training for the race. Anything I can get you from the city?"

"Chapstick?"

"Always the smart-ass."

The crush of gravel warned of a truck approaching on its way to the village. "I better go," Kerry said. He blew me another kiss and pushed off into the night.

I floated down the lane to Grams', not worried at all about the wildlife, or Mike and Barb, or world peace, or Sam and Elizabeth, or global warming, or whether or not I'd ever be able to call myself a writer.

That night, I worried only about how I'd be able to leave Lake Ringrose when the summer was over.

Chapter Twenty

"Aren't you afraid the paint fumes will give us brain damage?" I laughed three days, eleven hours, and twenty minutes later—but who was counting. Grams and I had finished the walls; now she'd started me on shelves, end tables, old chests. No surface was safe from me and my paintbrush.

Grams studied me. "You're awfully cheerful this afternoon."

Okay, so I couldn't get the grin off my face. I should have warned Kerry that I was as good as *Entertainment Tonight* at keeping secrets. Even if I didn't actually say anything, something always gave me away. But I'd recently received another express letter from Sam. Grams assumed that alone was responsible for my perma-grin, though honestly, I didn't know what to think about Sam's letter. He'd weirded out on me.

> *. . . Charlie, I thought having a girlfriend would be more exciting than sitting in cafés with textbooks spread out on the tabletop. Can I really call Elizabeth my girlfriend if she hasn't kissed me yet? Liz's college friends stop by sometimes to gawk at me—her Canadian "mate"—like I'm some sort of rare and*

exotic giraffe. They ask why I'm not at the "uni" with
them (I told them I'm taking time off from the "uni"
back in Canada). A few have given me odd looks, no
doubt recognizing me for the "ratbag" that I am. I've
been thinking about growing a goatee; will that
make me look older?

Charlie, I miss hanging around someone who real-
ly knows where I come from—not just what I've told
them. Someone who doesn't make me wait a half-
hour on a bench in a crowded mall while she goes to
reapply her eyeliner and mascara and lip-goop. I
don't get the makeup thing. I've seen you with bed
head and eye-crusts and still thought you were pretty.
I can bet that Kerry guy thinks you're pretty, too. Has
he made a move? Sorry, I suppose I have no right to
feel so . . . I don't know.
Write again soon,
Sam

I'd sat on the steps of the post office and scribbled a reply
to Sam's letter on the back of a fishing derby flyer.

Sam?
I recognize the handwriting but . . . are you feel-
ing okay?
Pretty? Pretty what? I'm waiting for the punchline,
Sam. Pretty ugly? Pretty gullible? You've called me
many things over the years: Frizzyhead, Charlie the
Tuna, or my personal favorite—not!—Beluga Butt.
But pretty? Have you recently had a blow to the head?
When did it occur to you that I was even a girl?

trist

Now about this Liz creature. Don't wait for her to make a move. Catch her off guard and kiss her. That's my two cents (Canadian) worth. Go for the gut. Don't get all technical and over-analytic. Don't hesitate and give her time to duck. How she responds will tell you if it's your whole person she likes, or just your free tutorials. If she gags or slaps you, it's probably a bad sign, but don't take it as a reflection of your kissing skills; after all, you played sax in the band. And skip the goatee; it will definitely make you look older—like forty!

In answer to your other question: yes, Kerry made a move. I don't know if it's so much that he likes me as that I'm the only female in town over the age of twelve and under thirty-five. We have fun together, but we can talk seriously, too—something you and I never did easily, at least not face-to-face.

I have a question for you, too. Let's say Liz lets you kiss her and there are these earth-moving fireworks and your relationship becomes the stuff of a nauseating Savage Garden love song. What happens when you have to leave? How do you say goodbye? Chew on that awhile,

Charlie.

All the while I was writing, out of the corner of my eye, I could see Jenny watching me from the window of the café next door. Part of me wanted to stick my tongue out at her. The other part of me wanted to say something nice to her, to find a way to dig through her frosty layers to see what goodness must lie somewhere inside her.

After all, she was the woman who had given birth to Kerry.

Seven hours and forty-one minutes later, Kerry showed up on Grams' kitchen doorstep late in the afternoon with a two-liter tub stuffed with fresh raspberries.

"Hey, you." He grinned.

I stifled the urge to throw my arms around him.

Grams' head popped up from salad she was mixing for dinner. Her face lit up when she saw the fruit. "You picked them yourself?"

"On my way over. First of the season," Kerry replied.

"Let me pay you." Grams wiped her hands on her jeans and reached for her purse. She pulled out a ten.

He waved her money away. "I won't take it, Josie. How about feeding me some of whatever is simmering on your stove instead?"

Over chicken stew and whole wheat rolls, Kerry told us that Doc Will had gone to Wawa to meet his bus from Sault Ste. Marie. On the bumpy ride back to Lake Ringrose, he'd cajoled Kerry into organizing the Labour Day Weekend wharf dance. "I need a theme," he said. "Any ideas?"

"What was the theme last summer?" I asked.

"The Wild West. The year before was Hooray for Hollywood—everyone dressed as their favorite movie stars. Josie got vamped up like Julia Roberts."

Grams swatted his arm. "*I did not!* I went as Lucille Ball."

Kerry flexed his biceps and did a hopeless Terminator impersonation. "I went as Arnold Schwarzenegger."

"Doc Will went as Harrison Ford. Indiana Jones—now *there's* a leading man," Grams said.

"Care to elaborate?" Kerry chided her. He nudged my leg under the table with his foot.

Trist

Blushing, Grams changed the subject. "Would you consider an Eighties theme, Kerry? There are all those old music and video cassettes in Geri's room; she used to drive her father crazy with her loud music at all hours. I think the stereo still works. You could hook it up to the big speakers at the village hall." Grams turned to me. "Your mother always loved to party."

Well, there was one gene I didn't inherit.

Later, Kerry and I sorted through Geri's music collection. Sprawled on her bedroom floor, we listened to Culture Club, Depeche Mode, Loverboy, Duran Duran, Thompson Twins, and soundtracks from the movies *Fame* and *Flashdance* before agreeing Grams might be on to something.

"Why don't we organize an air band contest?" Kerry suggested, rifling through another pile of cassettes. "Lots of the villagers are in their thirties and forties now—they'd know this stuff. Doug at the general store might donate some prizes. Alex is always willing to chip in a rod and some lures. Even Mom might toss in a few day-old pies if we catch her on a good day."

"Since when did planning this dance planning 'our' job?" I asked.

Kerry checked left and right for the Grams Patrol, then gave me a quick kiss. "Since it became another excuse for you and me to spend time together," he whispered.

Three cheers for teamwork.

We listened to more music. Geri had a huge collection: Bryan Adams, Adam Ant, Rod Stewart, Supertramp, Chris de Burgh, Phil Collins, Rush, Eurythmics, Van Halen, Foreigner, Lionel Richie, Wham! It would take us *days* to sort through it all.

While I jotted our ideas for the dance on notebook paper, Kerry drummed his fingers on his knees in time to the music and flipped distractedly through Geri's sketchbook that I'd left on the bedside table.

"Nice drawings," he exclaimed, closing the book and putting it aside to change cassettes. "I especially like the sketch of my dad and me fishing."

It took a few seconds for what Kerry had said to raise red flags. Tossing aside the dance plans, I grabbed the sketchbook and turned to the last drawing.

"What sketch of you and your dad? This is the last drawing." I pointed to the deer eating leaves. "See the date? Geri was seventeen. How could there have been a drawing of you and your dad? Weren't your parents and my mother all the same age?"

Kerry took the book from me and continued flipping, past about fifteen blank pages, until another series of sketches appeared, sketches I'd overlooked all those times I'd examined the sketchbook myself. Sure enough, there was a pencil sketch of a man and a tiny boy dressed in bathing suits fishing off a dock.

"What makes you think that's you and your dad?" The figures were really just specks against a landscape.

"That's our dock." Kerry pointed. "See the A-frame poking out of the trees? And look at the angle of our bodies. Dad was teaching me to cast—I still have that toy rod somewhere. I couldn't have been more than a year or two old."

"I bet you were a cute kid."

"Now I'm Frankenstein."

"You are not," I replied, still distracted by the sketchbook. The date on the drawing of Kerry and his father wasn't right.

It couldn't be right. It was dated the summer after Geri and Mike were married, the summer they backpacked in Europe. There was even a photo of Mike and Geri in front of the Eiffel Tower on my desk back home.

I flipped more pages. There were more drawings. Grams weeding the garden. Two grizzled old men paddling a canoe. The old barn—Brian Baker's studio—where I found the sketchbook. All dated improperly. I flipped a few more pages and sucked in my breath. Oh. My. God.

It was the Chocolate Moose Man.

His face wasn't visible, but my mother had drawn the over-the-shoulder portrait as he whittled a stick—I just knew it was him. I recognized the Chocolate Moose Man's hands and the scary skull ring on his pinky. I could almost smell his worn leather jacket. The back of his head, covered by a turned-up collar and baseball cap gave me no clues to his identity. But something about his posture seemed familiar. Maybe Kerry knew. Was the Chocolate Moose Man here at Lake Ringrose? Had I met him in the village and not known it?

"Kerry?" I held up the book for him. "Do you know who—"

Grams barged in, interrupting. "I'm heading to bed now," she said. "It's past eleven. Time for you to skedaddle, Mr. Sanderson."

I closed the sketchbook and walked Kerry to the porch. "We'll begin serious training for the Four Islands Race tomorrow," he said, giving my hand a squeeze. He walked across the lawn to his bike, then turned back. "You were about to show me something before? About the sketchbook?"

"It wasn't important," I said, waving as Kerry flipped on his headlamp and cycled into the night. Now wasn't the time to get into it; I had enough potential grist in my life. No need to dwell on cloudy memories from my preschool days.

Even so, that night I dreamed of moose.

Chapter Twenty-One

August arrived and the weather stayed warm and dry. Since I'd painted everything but the kitchen sink (literally!), I spent more time during the long, lazy days working on my journal. Mr. Pollen used to say that grist-gathering was like collecting the pieces of a jigsaw puzzle, and that writing was about putting the pieces together in an intelligent and entertaining way. I wondered if the product of that summer's grist would turn out to be a simplistic pre-school puzzle, or if it might take on the properties of a two-thousand-piece 3D puzzle, complete with working parts.

Most evenings, Kerry dropped by after dinner and we'd train for the Four Islands Race. Our sessions would begin with a half-hour swim followed by power-paddling in zigzag patterns across the lake. (Kerry insisted, and I stupidly didn't doubt him, that his roundabout canoe routes were designed only to keep us out of the wake of powerboats.) Three times a week, he also had me sprawled on Grams' dock lifting free weights and doing push-ups to strengthen my upper body. When I looked in Grams' full-length bathroom mirror, I hardly recognized myself anymore. I saw the body of one of those jock girls I'd always envied, not Charlie the Pear.

And I liked it.

Kerry insisted that the training was good for him, too, that it counted as physiotherapy. He said that his legs were getting stronger, that they didn't ache so much after biking to the tree house or climbing ladders. Despite this, he still couldn't run more than fifty feet at a time. His chances of making it back onto his old minor hockey team in the fall were zilch, but he could swim like a barracuda, and paddle for over an hour against the wind without a break. He had high hopes that if we pushed ourselves, we could place well in the Four Islands Race. Earlier on in our training, I'd humored Kerry when he spoke like that. Now I was right there with him, looking forward to putting my new muscles to the test. It surprised me that I was capable of putting so much effort into the training. Into anything.

And I liked that, too.

Despite all the extra time we spent together training for the race and planning the wharf dance, Grams hadn't warned me again about "keeping my distance" from Kerry. I felt bad betraying her. Felt guilty that each race-training session was followed by a make-out session at Kerry's back lot or on one of the small uninhabited islands he felt I should "tour" before race day. But I couldn't see how having Kerry for a boyfriend could be a bad thing; he was good-looking, outdoorsy, and we could argue and laugh for hours. And when it came to messing around, unlike with the canoeing and swimming and push-ups, Kerry never cajoled me to go further or do more than I wanted. On the other hand, any time I attempted to scale the barbed-wire fence surrounding my comfort zones, he was more than happy to cheer me on.

"Did you just slide your hand over my left butt cheek, Charlie-girl?" he laughed one day.

"I'm sorry," I squeaked. Mortified, I snatched my hand back.

Kerry hooted, took my hand, and placed it back over his rear pocket. "I love you," he whispered into my hair.

I backed up. I couldn't believe my ears. "You *what?*"

"You heard me."

I hugged Kerry hard, mumbled a few words into his chest. Kerry laughed. "Say that again?"

I looked him in the eye. "I love you, too."

The second week of August, I received yet another express letter from Australia. I'd soon have quite a stamp collection.

> *Hey Charlie!*
>
> *I took your lousy advice. Be glad I'm several continents away, because if I could, I'd strangle you—or at least fill your bed with spiders.*
>
> *I kissed Elizabeth. She didn't exactly PUKE, but it's over. Coincidentally, so are her mid-terms. She told me she just wasn't into getting "serious" with anyone right now, like I'd asked her to marry me or something? (By the way, what did you mean about me being a good kisser because I played the sax? I sucked at the sax. Don't you remember I dropped music last semester because it was bringing down my grade-point average?) Charlie, I wish I was twelve again and my biggest social worry was that my pits smelled.*
>
> *In answer to your question, I knew you were a girl the summer between sixth and seventh grades. Wearing a baggy Senators T-shirt over your bathing suit didn't*

fool anyone; you were growing "norks" as the Aussies call them. My mom said if I teased you about it she'd kill me—or worse, take away my computer. So I pretended like I didn't notice, and you never said anything when I started to grow red fuzz on my lip the summer after. Maybe it was just our way of keeping "Charlie and Sam" the same even while you and I were changing. Maybe it was a bad idea.

Dad's got a meeting with his boss tomorrow. His contract is going to be extended. Maybe for another year. Maybe more. I have to make a big decision about school. There's a test I can write to make me eligible to skip my senior year of high school and begin courses here at the "uni" next semester. I know I always said I wanted to go to university in Ottawa, but it's a chance to start my career that much sooner.

What should I do?

Sam

Late that night, I sat on Grams' porch swing with a pen and paper and tried to respond to Sam's letter. But I didn't know what to say. Since kindergarten, Sam had been hell-bent on becoming a computer graphics specialist. A real friend would encourage him to stay in Australia and go to the "uni." To find his niche in the Australian computer world. To earn a cool ten million by his twenty-first birthday. But the thought of never seeing him again—or not for a very, *very* long time—was making me hyperventilate, was making my bottom lip quiver. How selfish was it that even though I had my own boyfriend now, I still wanted to be the most important female in Sam's life?

"Everything okay?" Grams asked from the hammock. She was flipping through the latest *People* magazine.

I forced my rancid emotions back inside where they belonged. "Sam's family is staying in Australia."

"For another year?"

"Forever." I might as well get used to it.

"The world's not as big as it used to be, Charlena. You'll see him again."

"I don't think so."

She put her magazine aside. "I felt the same way, Charlena, when Geri called your gramps and me at the end of her third year of university to tell us that she was getting married and moving to Springdale. We missed her so much already, I couldn't come to grips with the thought of her never coming home again, except to visit. Maybe that's why I saved all her old high school stuff—to keep pieces of her with me. Then, when she passed away, I just couldn't bring myself to put it all away. I know it's silly; it's just *stuff*. You're the only real part of Geri I have left." Her eyes glistened.

I got up and kissed Grams' cheek and told her how glad I was that she'd invited me to stay at Lake Ringrose that summer. "After Mike and Geri were married, did she ever come back here to visit?" I asked, curious to know if Grams could shed light on that last series of drawings. If the dates were true, there was no way that the sketchbook could have been left behind in Brian Baker's studio when Geri'd stormed out of her tutorial at age seventeen. But how could it have been left there the summer after she and Mike were married, the summer they were supposedly in Europe? Something was fishy.

But Grams was vague. "Not as often as your gramps and I would have liked. But we spoke often on the phone. When you were a tiny baby, before she got sick, Geri'd call us every evening while you were crying. She'd put the phone up to your little ear and I'd sing you lullabies. Darn if they didn't put you right to sleep."

"I used to *cry* when I was a baby?"

"Of course," Grams laughed. "Healthiest lungs on the street, according to Mike."

Chapter Twenty-Two

Two weeks before the Labour Day weekend, Grams went to Wawa with Doc Will after dinner to play in a seniors softball tournament, a fund-raiser for the Cancer Society. I'd wanted to go along to watch, but Grams insisted I'd be bored to death. I was more inclined to think that Grams and the doctor just didn't want me along.

Before Doc Will arrived, I'd caught Grams in the kitchen dabbing on lipstick.

"Grams?" She started, quickly shoving the lipstick tube into her purse. "Are you and Doc Will a couple?"

"A couple of what?"

"A couple of . . . you know . . . a *couple.*"

Her face turned crimson. "Heavens, no. Your gramps would roll over in his grave. What gave you a crazy idea like that? Don't go getting all imaginative on me."

But when Doc Will arrived at the door carrying a single daisy he'd plucked from the lane, held the door for her, and said, "After you, my dear," Grams giggled like a sixth-grader and wouldn't meet my eye as she followed him out to his truck. Were they really going to a softball game? Did people over sixty have sex? Sick.

Not long after they left, Kerry arrived at the doorstep in a foul mood. "Hey, you," he growled.

"What's wrong?" I pulled him into the kitchen to keep out the bees.

He slammed his motorcycle helmet onto the counter; he'd finally found the ATV keys—hidden in Jenny's recipe box. "Just another fight with Mom."

"Just another fight" didn't make him slam things around. "What happened?" I asked.

"I spent the morning today, from six to noon, splitting logs at the Trevertons'. Then I spent the afternoon digging a drainage ditch at the Jollettes'. I got home around five, took a shower, then committed the federal offense of laying down on the couch to rest my legs."

"We don't have to train tonight," I said. "Grams isn't here. We could make popcorn and watch old videos or something."

"I'd like that."

"But first tell me what happened with your mother."

Kerry groaned. "Why do you always want to hear this stuff? Nobody else ever wants to hear it."

"I'd like to think I'm not 'nobody' for starters. Is there anything I can do to help?"

He laughed darkly. "Know a good hit man?"

I went to the fridge and took out a pitcher of iced tea. Poured us both a glass. Pulled out two chairs at the kitchen table. Gestured for Kerry to sit. "Was it something she said?"

Kerry took a long swallow of tea and began to rant. "Mom came home from the café around six, in a putrid mood, bitching that the new snack bar over at the beach is stealing all her business. Then she started in on me. Screaming about how dare I spend my day sleeping on the couch when she has to slave over a hot oven trying to conjure up enough business to pay the store's mortgage? She'll never let me forget that she had to re-mortgage the shop to pay for Dad's funeral and his bad debts and legal costs. She acts like she doesn't remember that I gave her my life savings—almost forty grand—my cabin money—every bloody cent I've earned since I was twelve—to help her out. She never even said thanks. Took it like it was her due. Like I personally asked for everything that happened. Thank God for OHIP; she'd have probably let me die before she forked over a cent for my medical treatment."

So that was why Kerry worked so many jobs, and why people were always trying to tip him for favors. They *knew.* "You must have had some pretty hefty legal bills, too."

"I was represented by a public defender. The guy couldn't have been out of law school more than two weeks. Mom said if I wanted better, Lisa and I could sell the back lot. Lisa was all for it; she thinks that the only way we can rise above our crappy family legacy is to escape. To get the hell out. But I'll never give up the pond. I *love* it here. Look at your grandparents, and Doc Will, and those other folks who've lived at Lake Ringrose their entire lives. They've managed to build nice homes and find work and keep up with the times. They haven't sprouted horns. They didn't all become alcoholics or drug addicts or adulterers or criminals, right?"

"You're not your father, Kerry."

"Damn right, I'm not my father!" He pounded his fist on the table. "But tell that to my mother. She's been mad at my father ever since I can remember. He's dead, and she's *still* mad at my father, maybe even more so this summer."

"Why?"

"Beats me. But it's like every time she sees *me,* she sees *him.* Sometimes I'll look up from a magazine or my dinner plate and catch her glaring at me."

Kerry looked down at his knuckles. One was swollen and cut up. "Tonight I couldn't take it anymore. I told her to fuck off. Right before I put my fist through the living room wall."

Grams had warned me, had told me Kerry was hanging by a thread. Maybe she'd been right after all. I couldn't take my eyes off Kerry's hands, the ones I'd only ever associated with strength and gentleness. The fact they were capable of violence made me a bit nauseous.

"I'm kicked out of the house. For good, this time. Mom says I'm eighteen, I own a piece of 'swamp,' so I can just bloody well spend the rest of my crippled life there in the tree house for all she cares."

"But it'll be below zero at night in another month!"

Kerry shrugged. "The Doc might let me stay on his couch in exchange for working on his truck or something. Just until I get enough money saved to build my cabin on the back lot."

"Maybe your mom will come around," I suggested.

"Not bloody likely. Besides, she's right; I'm eighteen. An adult. It's time I was independent."

"But you gave her all your money!"

"So I'll make more. Don't worry about me, Charlie-girl; I'm upset now, but I'll be fine on my own. I'll miss you, though, when you have to go home. I can't believe the summer's over in a couple of weeks."

I wasn't looking forward to leaving, either. I missed Mike like crazy, but did I want to go home to a family that might include Barb and her three large pieces of boy-baggage? Mike hadn't mentioned Barb at all during his phone calls recently; he no doubt figured that I couldn't make snide remarks about her if he didn't set them up first with all his gushy compliments. If he'd popped the big one, it was still news to me. Mike was probably saving the bad news until I got home.

"Think you'll stay in touch?" Kerry asked, calmer now. "I'd hate if we broke up over a few hours drive."

"It's *fourteen* hours. And you don't have a car."

"Maybe I could come on the bus with your Grams in October. Didn't she say the other night that she was still planning her Thanksgiving trip to Springdale?"

"Yes!" I exclaimed. "But, wait. Aren't we supposed to be a secret?"

Kerry shook his head. "I don't care what my mother thinks right now. And Josie won't really mind, will she? I know she probably thinks I'm too old for you, or too much of a country hick, but—"

"We'll tell Grams when she gets home tonight." She'd just have to accept that I was responsible enough to handle the relationship. I *had* been handling it just fine, thank you very much.

"What about that Sam guy, the Irish Setter?" Kerry asked.

What a laugh; Kerry jealous of Sam. "Sam is staying in Australia," I said. "And I *told* you, Kerry, he's just a friend." Besides, once Sam started going to the "uni" in Canberra, he'd forget all about me. There'd be oodles of girls attracted to his super-sized intellect and Ottawa Valley accent. His weekly correspondence with me would dwindle to a yearly Christmas card—if I was lucky.

"Maybe if you come down to see me at Thanksgiving, my father will let me come up here for Christmas," I said. The thought of sharing Christmas with Barb and her three goblins wasn't nearly as festive as that of spending the holiday here with Grams and Kerry. I felt more mature already, just making these plans. Grams would see that Kerry was right for me. Damn near perfect. "And I'll e-mail you every day," I added.

"Could you write letters instead?" Kerry asked. "I don't have a computer and I don't trust the Internet service at the community school. I don't want some horny twelve-year-old hacking into my x-rated mail."

"X-rated?"

"Yeah," Kerry grinned. "Write me some of that stuff you'd like to do but don't have the guts for."

"I'm getting more gutsy."

He laughed. "Promises, promises."

Kerry and I finished our tea and found ourselves on the couch in the den with the benign intention of watching one of Geri's VHS tapes, *Footloose*. But when Kerry got up and began a spastic Kevin Bacon dance impersonation, I fell back on the couch laughing. He fell on top of me and well, things cut loose.

We came up for air a while later. Kerry raised an eyebrow at me. "You think before you leave this summer . . ."

Yikes. I should have known the sex question would be tabled before the end of the summer. Kerry was eighteen, a *man*, for God's sake. His virginity was probably just a distant junior high memory.

"I, uh, don't think I'm ready," I said, sounding like the dopey heroine in some lame sex-ed video.

"Your body says it's ready."

"It's the rest of me that's the hard sell."

"No problem," Kerry said. "We'll just keep it as something to look forward to. There's no rush. Don't give me that skeptical look, Charlie-girl. It's been more than eight months for me now and I haven't died yet."

"You haven't gone blind either."

He laughed. "Not for lack of trying. Maybe if I channel all that horny energy into my school work this fall, I'll actually pass history and French."

"Just don't fall in love with your French teacher." All I needed was another Madame Dumas in my life.

"With *Mr.* Duncan?"

"Forget I said anything."

"Let's not say anything for awhile."

More heavy breathing and rolling around. My body was sending my head an urgent message to re-think the sex thing. The fact Kerry wasn't being pushy about it made me more open to the idea of actually doing it. If it was a ploy, it was a good one.

"Kerry? I've been thinking . . . maybe—"

"AHHHHHHHHHHH!"

Shitshitshitshitshitshitshit!!!!!

Why was Grams back so soon?

Why had *Footloose* run its final credits, leaving the room bathed in white noise? My cheeks felt raw from Kerry's beard stubble. Had we been making out for—*three hours?*

Kerry jumped off me and grabbed his shirt off the floor where he'd flung it. I leaped up and struggled to pull myself together.

I was pretty competent at reading facial expressions, but once the initial shock of seeing Kerry and I tangled up on the couch had passed, Grams' was indecipherable. I expected anger, disgust, mortification, but she seemed none of those. Only sad, perhaps resigned.

Still standing in the doorway, her voice barely a whisper, she asked Kerry—politely—to leave. "Will's got a load of firewood in the back of his truck; maybe you could follow him back to town? Give him a hand with it?"

Kerry flipped off the TV, nodded apologetically to Grams, gave me a little embarrassed wave, and left. The room was silent except for the pounding in my chest and the look in Grams' eyes, which spoke volumes, but in a language I couldn't comprehend. What the hell was happening?

"Grams," I started, "Kerry and I were just messing around."

She walked over and stood next to me. "I know."

I tried for damage control. "Well, don't look so worried. It's no big deal. I know I told you I'd keep my distance, but you *know* Kerry. He's a great friend. It's not like we were—"

Well, not yet, anyway.

Grams shook her head. "It can't continue."

"But—"

"You don't understand. Kerry's not right for you."

"Look," I huffed. "I know about his past—the drugs and parties and girls—but he's changed. Kerry's trying to get his life together. To move on."

"I know, Charlena. And I don't object to you being friends. I've told you that again and again and again. But I *also* said that you MUST keep your distance. I thought we had an understanding. It's just not right."

"*What's not right about it!* I'm sorry, and really embarrassed, that you saw us like that on the couch, but—" I took a deep breath, tried to control my anger. Maybe reasoning was the answer. "Didn't *you* have a boyfriend when you were sixteen?"

Grams sighed deeply, sunk down on the couch, motioned for me to sit next to her. I didn't want to—not until we had our differences sorted out—but she wasn't asking. I sat.

"Yes, Charlena," Grams responded after a long pause. "I had a boyfriend when I was sixteen. I'm not so old that I don't remember what it's like to be young and in love. And if you were 'messing around' as you call it with some other boy here at the lake, that would be fine with me—to a certain degree. But not with Kerry."

"What's wrong with Kerry!"

"Nothing is *wrong* with him! But he's—" Grams stopped, examined her fingernails like she'd never noticed them before. A tear rolled down her cheek. "Dear God," she said to the ceiling. "I need Mike here to help me. I never thought it would come to this. I promised him everything would be okay. Will he ever forgive me?"

"TELL ME!" I didn't know if Grams' emotions were scaring me or just making me furious. Either way, I was tired of playing games. If there was something going on with Kerry I wanted to hear it. Anything was better than the same old mysterious warnings and insinuations.

Grams voice was hoarse. "Kerry's your brother."

Chapter Twenty-Three

Dead silence for a count of ten or more while I tried—unsuccessfully—to digest Grams' words. "My *what?*" I finally asked. I must have heard wrong.

"Kerry is your brother. Your half-brother."

My guts churned like the insides of a septic tank. I started blathering like an idiot. "You're telling me Geri had another baby here at Lake Ringrose? Two babies? What about Lisa?"

Grams face was pale beneath her tan. "Geri only ever had you. Jenny Sanderson is Lisa's and Kerry's mother."

"Then Mike had a baby with Jenny?" That made no sense.

Grams took my hand. "Greg Sanderson was your biological father."

What? I pushed her hand away. *"THAT'S A LIE!"* I screamed. *"Mike is my father!"*

Grams shook her head. Tears flooded her eyes.

I had to get out of there. I stood up. Shoved on my sneakers. Made for the door. What was that stupid mantra of Barb's? Oh yeah: *When the going gets tough, the tough get going.* That was me—going!

"Charlena, please," Grams begged. "You wanted to know. Let me try to explain."

I stood frozen in the doorway a few seconds. Then slowly, I turned back to face the woman who had just destroyed my life. All I wanted to hear was that I was only having a nightmare.

Grams reached for my hand again. She pulled me back down onto the couch. With her free hand, she plucked a tissue from the box on the coffee table and blew her nose.

"Well?" I demanded. Dread oozed from every pore.

Grams tightened her grip on my hand. "The summer you were . . . conceived . . . Mike was offered a once-in-a-lifetime opportunity to finish his last semester of business school in Europe. He was so excited. Thought he and your mother could have a real honeymoon."

"So what the hell happened?"

"Geri had just started her final nursing practicum at Glenside Hospital in Springdale. She didn't want to postpone the placement; she thought it might lead to full-time work."

"They split up?" I asked, aghast.

Grams nodded. "There were so many conflicts over what to do that they each went their own way. They were in love, but they were so young, Charlena. Not even finished university. Too immature in many ways to be settling down."

Whatever. "That doesn't explain how Geri ended up at Lake Ringrose that summer," I said.

"Geri's practicum at Glenside didn't work out. Some administrative glitch to do with the nurses' union; all the students were told to find new placements. She was still so upset with Mike for leaving her that she came back to Lake Ringrose. Got her credits doing house calls with Doc Will."

So, that explained the last series of sketches; Geri *had* been at the lake the summer after she and Mike were married. "But Greg Sanderson was married by then," I explained to Grams, as if I could somehow imply misunderstanding of the situation on her part. "He had two kids already. Lisa and Kerry were just babies. What was he thinking, hooking up with Geri?"

Grams frowned. "Takes two to tango."

I was appalled. Mike raised me to think my mother was perfect. A saint. Sweet, kind, funny, generous, feisty. Not a *skank* who would sleep with a married man, the father of two small children.

Grams sighed. "I only know two things. Greg was Geri's first big crush back in high school, so maybe she still carried feelings for him. And Greg, despite being married, had what used to be called 'a wandering eye'."

"Wandering *dick* is more like it! You knew what was going on?"

"Of course not!" Grams replied. "It wasn't until the fall, when Geri found out that she was three months pregnant, that she confided in me. Admitted that she and Greg slept together, just once, after the village Canada Day party. Said that all the young people had been pretty drunk that night. Jenny had fought with Greg earlier in the evening and had stomped off home. Greg and Geri got talking and went off somewhere. One thing led to another and . . . you know."

"No! I don't *know.*" Now I probably never would. Jesus, what if Kerry and I had . . . How would I ever look him in the face again? I sunk further into the couch cushion, wishing it were quicksand.

Grams sighed. "To her credit, I suppose, Geri came to her senses after that one . . . encounter. She knew that she was only one of many women being played by Greg Sanderson that summer. That messing around behind Mike's back—the man she loved and married—with the husband of a child-hood friend, no less—was just stupid. That Greg had enough bad habits to sink a freighter."

"Like not using a condom!"

Grams patted my shoulder. "You, Sweetie, were the best thing to come out of the whole mess."

Best for who? I shook her off. "How did Geri and Mike end up back together?" Just saying Mike's name out loud froze my tongue and burned my mouth simultaneously.

Grams answered. "Right after Canada Day, well before she ever suspected that she was pregnant, Geri rushed through her practicum hours with Doc Will, swallowed her pride, and took a plane to Europe to find Mike. She had no idea that he'd also rushed through his studies and was returning to Springdale to beg Geri to take him back." Grams chuckled. "It was like something out of those goofy romantic comedies on TV: missed connections, crossed wires, but in the end, true love and a week backpacking in France. I've seen that photo of them by the Eiffel Tower that you have on your desk back home; there was never any doubt in my mind that when Mike and Geri reunited, it would be forever."

"Forever only lasted another four years."

"Forever in their hearts."

I felt like puking. "That's a lie. If it were true, how could Geri lie to Mike? Let him think that I was his daughter?"

Grams gulped. She spoke slowly. "Mike knows about Greg, Charlena. He's known all along. He legally adopted you the day you were born."

The room was spinning. I clenched my eyes and wished myself away. Mike wasn't my father. He knew he wasn't my father. He'd been lying to me all these years.

"Greg didn't want me, I gather?" I finally spat.

"It was more complicated than that," Grams explained. "Geri didn't want to spend her life with Greg—not that Greg would have left Jenny anyway. He said he'd try to support you financially, if necessary, but that—"

"Why didn't she just get an abortion?"

"Because she wanted you. She was determined to have you and keep you, even knowing that the truth about her pregnancy might split her and Mike up permanently. She said if Mike forced her to choose between you and him, she'd choose you. Never forget that, Charlena. And don't forget that Mike agreed to love you and raise you as his own. And he has, despite everything. Mike would give his life for you, you know that!"

Yeah, yeah. I threw my head back, wishing the couch cushions were made of cement. "No wonder Jenny's been so cold to me."

Grams laughed bitterly. "Charlena, Jenny is cold to everyone; you've been here long enough to know that."

"She has every right to be angry with me."

"Charlena, she's not mad at you, not really. She's mad at herself."

"Huh?"

Grams sighed. "It's sad what happened to Jenny Sanderson. She was such a vivacious teenager, had dreams of being a famous dancer, or an actress on Broadway. She left Lake Ringrose the day after her graduation from the community school with her sights set on New York City. She arrived back at the lake six months later, cold and bitter. God only knows what kind of messes she got herself into; she's never spoken about them. But it was like all the life had been

Jrist

177

sucked out of her. She married Greg Sanderson a few months later, had Lisa and Kerry in quick succession. Jenny will tell anyone who'll listen that she hates the way her life has turned out. She hates that she married a lying, cheating fool. She hates that Lisa is smarter than she is. She hates that Kerry takes after his old man."

"No, he doesn't!" I yelled, my words on fire. It was like a fresh log had been tossed on my anger.

"He does in the good ways, Charlena. Kerry knows the land. He's a hard worker."

"Jenny only sees the bad things."

"Jenny just wants better for him than what she thinks Lake Ringrose has to offer. She's proud of Lisa for going to university, but I wonder if she's a little jealous, too, the way she was of Geri when she was accepted to university. Jenny's afraid that Kerry will end up feeling trapped here the way she does."

"He doesn't feel trapped. He loves it here!"

"You're preaching to the choir, Charlena."

I didn't need to ask if Jenny and my mother ever reconciled. Jenny was bitter to the core, even now, thirteen years after my mother's death. "I don't get how Jenny and Greg ever stayed together as long as they did."

"Jenny loved Greg as much as she hated him, maybe more. Or maybe she thought that he was the best she could do. And Greg loved that Jenny had a small inheritance to finance his rig. Their relationship wasn't ideal, but it was a relationship nevertheless. Not everybody has a fairytale marriage, Charlena. Not even your Gramps and I were perfect together."

Speaking of Gramps, "Weren't you and Gramps upset with Greg Sanderson after what happened?" I asked. "How could you all just go on living in the same tiny village knowing what had happened?"

"Your Gramps never knew about the affair," Grams said. "He was old-fashioned and had a bad heart. He assumed you were Mike's baby, and no one ever suggested otherwise; it would have killed him. Or," Grams smirked, "your gramps would have killed Greg. As for me, I don't hold grudges. Besides, I knew that Mike would be a great father. He loves kids."

Sure. Like Barb's. The triplets and I were on an even playing field. I wasn't anybody special. I wasn't Mike's flesh and blood. If Barb and Mike got married, I'd just go on being one of his social welfare projects.

"Did Greg ever ask about me?" My mouth was so dry.

Grams gave me a sad smile and nodded. "Whenever he had a chance, Greg asked about you, Charlena. As recently as last Christmas, just a week before he died, he dropped by to see your new school pictures. And—"

"I don't look like Kerry," I interrupted, still grasping at the possibility that everything might all be just a big misunderstanding. "Do I look like Lisa?"

Grams shook her head. "You look like Geri. Spitting image."

"Lucky for all of you, isn't it!"

Grams buried her head in her hands.

I chewed on my lip, not knowing what to say, not knowing if I wanted to say anything to anyone ever again. My swirling thoughts took me back to Brian Baker's ramshackle studio where I'd found Geri's sketchbook, to the dust and cobwebs, to the futon with the lumpy mattress. Had I been conceived there with those big painted moose looking on?

Did Brian know that Geri and Greg had been there? Kerry said his father had been hired to look after Brian's place one summer many years ago; had Greg been using the barn regularly with different women? Is *that* the reason for Brian and Greg's falling out? Had Geri left the sketchbook behind the night of her tryst? Is *that* why Brian kept the book all those years instead of returning it to Grams? Or had he simply tossed the book aside and never given it a second thought?

None of that mattered now.

"Was anyone *ever* going to tell me about this?" I finally asked.

Grams wiped her eyes. "Geri and Mike planned to tell you when you were old enough to understand, but after your mother got sick, Mike said he thought it was better to just leave it alone. I think he needed you to belong to him as much as you needed him to be your dad."

I could still taste Kerry's lips on my mouth, feel his hands on my body. I wasn't dead, but I could feel maggots crawling inside me. "So *that's* why I've never been invited to spend time here before!" Forget that bullshit about phone lines and "splendid fall colors."

"It would have been so complicated having you here," Grams explained. "Lisa and Kerry don't know about you—Jenny made sure of it—though I suppose they'll need to be told now. And I was always afraid after Geri died that Greg—if he got to know you—would challenge the adoption and make trouble for you and Mike."

"But it's okay now," I yelled, "because the man who fathered me is dead, my half-sister is away at university, and my half-brother was supposed to be too messed up with his own problems to notice me!"

Grams sighed deeply. "Charlena, I always regretted that you never got a chance to know Lisa and Kerry when you were all children. Especially when your mother died and Mike took so long to begin dating again. Your gramps and I always hoped that he'd re-marry, that he'd give you siblings."

"I had Sam."

"But friends come and go. Family is . . . well, it's family."

I fell in love with my half-brother. We kissed and touched and . . . eewwwwww. I cringed, shuddered at what might have happened eventually if Grams hadn't caught up with us. It was all my fault; if I'd only done what Grams asked and kept my distance, none of this would have happened. Now *I had a half-sister who I'd never laid eyes on.* And the biggest bomb: *Mike, my sweet, dorky dad, wasn't my biological father.* The reality of the situation was sinking in and the whole room went spinning again, my past blurring.

I rose on shaky legs. "I need some air."

Grams gripped my arm. "Charlena, you don't look well. You've had a terrible shock. Please sit down. Try to relax."

I shook Grams off again and headed for the door. "I'm going for a walk." There would be no stopping me this time.

Grams had aged in the last twenty minutes; her voice sounded eighty. "Not too far, Charlena," she called. "It's dark and overcast. *Please* don't run to Kerry about this; let me contact Jenny first. And I need to call Mike. I—"

Ignoring her, I grabbed a flashlight from the hook by the kitchen door and let the screen door slam behind me. I ran up the lane to the main road, then along the road, not towards the village, but the other way, towards—I hoped—oblivion. When the road ended, I turned again, onto a vaguely familiar, overgrown path and ran faster, tripping on

Trist

181

exposed roots and scratching my arms and face on branches. I kept running, in the thin beam of the flashlight, until there wasn't an ounce of air left in my lungs. Then I stumbled, gasping with exhaustion, against Brian Baker's old studio.

Slumped against the splintered barn board, the stress of the evening—of my life!—came crashing down on me like a bookshelf. Years worth of hot salty tears burned my face, sobs racked my ribcage, snot flowed like lava over my lips and chin.

Mr. Pollen could take his ideas about "grist" and shove them up his ass.

I cried and cried and cried, until my throat ached and my eyes swelled. Until the forest noises, which hadn't concerned me in weeks, closed in. Until a sudden burst of cold rain soaked me to the bone.

Shivering, I yanked open the rear hatch a few feet, crawled into the barn, and huddled in a ball on the cold floor, praying that Brian wouldn't choose that night to make a trip back to Lake Ringrose. I wondered if Kerry knew the terrible truth by now. Would he ever speak to me again? I dreaded seeing him, but I wanted him to know how sorry I was that everything had turned out so badly. I wanted him to hug me and tell me it was okay, that it was all just a weird, hallucinogenic episode brought on by paint fumes or too much water up my nose.

But in my heart, I knew that Grams was being truthful. From our first meeting down at the village wharf, I'd felt connected to Kerry. But our compatibility wasn't romantic; it was genetic. We didn't look alike, but Kerry and I could read each other's emotions like we were looking into a mirror. We understood each other's quirks and humor. Did Kerry have that with Lisa, too? Would she see my existence as just another reason to distance herself from Lake Ringrose? I bet Kerry and Lisa never made out to *Footloose.* Kerry and I were sick, a couple of perverts. Incest was such an ugly word.

Thinking about Mike brought on a fresh crop of tears. Poor Mike. All those times we fought, or I'd wished he was more grist-worthy, and there he was, raising me as best he could, a kid who wasn't even his. He must have hated me sometimes. I hated him for lying to me.

And what the hell was I supposed to feel for Greg Sanderson, my reckless biological father, the father who gave me up at birth? Kerry had loved him, still loved him. Would I have loved him, too, if I'd been given the opportunity to know him?

A mouse scuttled across the floor near my hand. I screamed. I couldn't lie there all night. The flashlight was fading, but I didn't bother feeling around for a light switch. I stumbled in the direction of the moose-muraled sleeping quarters and tripped onto the futon. Pulling the rough musty blanket around my damp shoulders, I curled into a fetal position.

Despite everything, I was lulled by the pitch dark and the static drone of rain against the barn roof.

I was asleep in minutes.

Chapter Twenty-Four

I awoke to sunlight streaming through cracks in the barn wall and the painted moose gazing at me with calm disinterest. Kerry was right; the wildlife mural wasn't frightening. It was peaceful, even. Or it *might* have been peaceful if my head wasn't so messed up. If it were possible to have an emotional hangover, I had a doozy that morning, and I knew a few Tylenols and a glass of orange juice wouldn't help one iota.

I groaned and rolled over. Then, *"AAAAAHHHHHHHH!"*

I wasn't alone.

Mike woke with a start. To a stranger he might have looked like a washed-out bum slumped over and drooling in the hardback chair he'd pilfered from Brian's kitchenette. Or like he'd just driven twelve hours straight from Toronto without a break, which I realized he must have. Mike wore wrinkled khaki shorts, a faded Blue Jays sweatshirt, and a ghostly pale complexion—the consequence of acute stress, road fatigue, and an indoor lifestyle.

To me, he looked . . . wonderful.

Before I could go through the maneuvers of stopping myself, I started bawling again.

Mike rushed over to the cot. He tried to hug me even as I pounded on his chest and screamed at him. "Liar! Get the hell away from me!" He kept kissing my hair and telling me that he loved me and that he was so sorry. That he should never have let me come to the lake. Or that he should have told me about Greg *before* letting me come to the lake. And that he should have spent more time with me the previous spring. That he should have bought me that horse I wanted back in fifth grade. I continued struggling and crying my eyes out. Mike was crying too—gut-wrenching, gasping sobs.

After a while, I calmed down and stopped hating Mike. I even thought I'd try to smile, to reassure him that I wasn't going to become homicidal or catatonic over the news of my parentage. But I ended up grimacing and hiccuping instead.

Mike extracted a rumpled tissue from his pocket and handed it to me. I used it first to dab at a blob of snot I'd inadvertently dribbled on his shoulder.

"Did Grams call and ask you to come up here?" I interrupted. "I'm sorry if she—"

Mike shushed me. "Char, I was in the car heading north before Josie finished saying hello; I could tell by her voice that something was wrong . . . . We really got ourselves into a mess this time, eh, kid?" he asked.

"But I'm not your kid," I sniffed. "Why did you put up with me all these years?"

"Char," Mike stared at me through shiny eyes. "Listen to me. Being your dad has been the greatest joy of my life."

And, suddenly, I knew it was true. Mike Conroy loved me. He gave me his name, had fed and clothed and housed me, let me wear his comfy old sweaters and didn't even get too freaked when I was thirteen and started tossing Tampax into the grocery cart. Mike's greatest fear in the world at that

Trist

185

moment was that the truth would divide us. That I would blame him. Reject him. Leave him.

"I love you, Mike," I said, throwing my arms around him. I felt years and years of stress drain from his body like pus from a wound. "Did Barb come with you?"

A shadow moved across Mike's face. "Barb and I broke up."

"You what?"

"Two weeks ago. I didn't tell you because I didn't want you to feel that you had to come to Toronto to console me. It sounded from your last few phone calls that you were really enjoying yourself here. Working hard. Keeping busy."

And messing around with my brother. "What happened?"

"We'll talk about Barb and me later," Mike said. "You and I need to get all this other stuff straightened out between us first."

Despite my initial anger, just having him there, I felt like I could breathe again for the first time in fourteen hours. The oxygen rush made me giddy. "Mike, we're straight. We're A-okay. In fact, I should be thankful; if I were your biological daughter, I'd have probably inherited your big nose."

"What? I love my nose."

I threw my arms around him again. "And it's not like I'll stop cutting the grass on Father's Day," I giggled, then started blubbering all over again. "I'm sorry." I wiped at my eyes angrily.

"Don't be sorry for crying, Char. You have every right."

"I hate crying. I always wanted to be tough for you."

"Forget being tough for me," Mike said. "Be strong—for yourself. Strong enough not to hide from your emotions."

My emotions. My heart was stewing in a gravy of horror, humiliation, confusion, fear, and . . . love. "Do you know if Kerry's okay?" I asked.

"It was Kerry who found you here last night," Mike said, wrapping his arm around my shoulder. "Josie said it took the two of them over two hours to find you. You weren't on the main road, or in the village, or at Kerry's tree house—*tree house?*—so he led her out here on a hunch. You were fast asleep and Josie didn't want to wake you. I arrived at Lake Ringrose about seven-thirty this morning. There was a note on Josie's door telling me to meet her here. She and I had a long talk when I arrived this morning. You had your Grams pretty worried running off like that."

"I can't believe Kerry helped her look for me. Does he . . . *know?*"

Mike nodded. "Josie thought it would be easier if he heard the truth from her, not his mother. They don't get along?"

"Jenny'll kill him!" I shouted. "What happened isn't all Kerry's fault, you know. It's mine, too. Grams tried to tell me that—"

"Char?"

"Yeah?"

"Nobody blames you or Kerry for what happened. Your Grams is blaming herself, but it's really *my* fault for not being honest with you years ago. You had a right to know the truth. I was just so afraid of what it would do to us. To me."

I started sniveling again, this time for Kerry, who despite having a crazy mother and now this stuff with me to contend with, had taken the time to help Grams out when she told him how upset I was, that I'd run off. The villagers, who only saw Kerry as the poor, undereducated general laborer, or the disabled ex-party-boy on probation, were missing the key element of what he was. Decent. They were missing the Kerry I fell in love with.

"Where's Grams now?" I asked, looking around.

"She walked home. Thought we'd need some time alone." He checked his watch. "It's almost ten now."

"Do you think Kerry's mad?" I couldn't get him out of my head.

Mike sighed. "I can bet he's understandably upset at the situation. I know it'll be awkward, but I hope the two of you will stay friends. Not everything has to change, Char."

"Just the messing around part," I mumbled, then shuddered. "God, what if he and I had . . ."

Mike grimaced. "Char, you're too young for that—with anybody."

"When *will* I be old enough, do you think?" I missed making Mike blush.

He didn't miss a beat. "When you're thirty."

I rolled my eyes. "Spoken like a true father."

"And don't ever forget it, kid."

I laid my head on his shoulder. "Mike?"

"Yeah, Char."

Kerry and I had never gotten around to making popcorn. "I'm starving."

Chapter Twenty-Five

After brunch with Grams, I took Mike on a leisurely two-hour paddle along the lakeshore. As best as he could, he explained what had happened between him and my mother the summer that I was conceived.

He also explained what had happened with Barb. How they'd just realized one day over lunch that besides a love of bowling and their kids, they had (Duh!!!!!!!) nothing in common. Mike just couldn't understand why Barb wanted to spend so much time at crowded malls and museums when all he wanted was to spend his down time doing the same things he'd have done back in Springdale: watching TV, eating pizza, reading spy novels. He never did pop the big one; instead of a ring, he'd bought new tires and a CD player for his mini-van. Barb had returned alone to her house in Ottawa to wait for the triplets to fly back from Vancouver.

Even a few days ago, I might have felt victorious. Now I felt kind of bad for Mike that things hadn't worked out for him. And I felt strangely sad for Matt, Rick, and Scott (it was safe now to acknowledge their real names); Mike would have been a good stepfather. I would have learned to deal with their obnoxious behaviors and smelly sports equipment sooner or later.

Or not.

"There's another woman out there for you, Mike," I said.

"I hope so."

"Don't wait another thirteen years to meet her, either," I added.

"Okay. And Char?"

"Yeah?"

"You won't have to wait thirteen years for the next guy, either."

I sobered. "Mike?"

He swiveled in the bow seat so that he was facing me, set his paddle across the gunwales, and gave me his full attention. It was like he knew that I was about to ask him *the* question. The one I rarely asked myself. The one I'd put off asking him for years because I was afraid of the answer.

I took a deep breath. "What if I get it all, Mike? The great guy. The best education. A fabulous writing career. And then . . . and then I get cancer, too?"

Mike sucked in his breath. Puffed out his cheeks like he was underwater. Finally, he surfaced. "Is *that* what you've been worrying about all these years?"

I shrugged. "I just always figured that if my life was dull and ordinary, if I didn't feel things too deeply, or try too hard at anything, that it wouldn't hurt so much to die young. I wouldn't know how much I was going to miss. Other people (you, Mike!) wouldn't miss me so much when I was gone." We were drifting out into the middle of the lake but I didn't care.

"Char, you know life doesn't work like that. There are no guarantees. Not for you, me, Geri, or anyone else."

"I know, I know, we could all get hit by a truck tomorrow. But—"

"It's no excuse not to make the most of the life you have!" Mike was emphatic. "It *is* a reason to work every day to pursue your dreams and follow your heart, even if in the end your life gets cut short. It took me a long time—*way too long*—to understand that."

"Did my mother understand it?" I asked.

"Geri always said that her biggest regret was that she gave up her dream of going to art school. That she was too proud and stubborn to take direction and criticism. She tried to make up for it those last months painting all those illustrations for the stories you told her. You couldn't even read or spell your name yet, but she knew—she knew!—that you'd want to be a writer someday. She wanted to encourage you as best she could." Mike looked up into the clouds as if for verification from Geri herself.

"Did she regret getting pregnant with me?"

"Maybe *how* it happened, but not that it did. She couldn't have known it at the time, but you were her first and last chance to have a baby. If she and I had waited a few years to start a family like we'd planned, it would have been too late. One of the last things your mother ever said to you was that you were her greatest work of art."

I picked up my paddle and turned us back towards shore. "I'm going to tell Grams not to sell the cottage," I announced. "Part of my life's here now."

Mike took in the scenery. "I might like spending a few weeks vacation here every summer."

"Vacation? You?"

Mike laughed. "It'll be good practice for my retirement."

Later that evening, I sat alone on the dock, my feet dangling in the lake. From a distance, I looked like the poster girl for serenity, but thoughts of Mike and Greg Sanderson consumed me. How would my life have been different if I'd known all along that Mike had adopted me? Was I spared heartache by never knowing my biological father, or did I miss my chance to develop a love of fishing? Was my past full of missed opportunities—missed "grist"—or should I just thank my lucky stars that Mike was always there for me?

"Hey, you. This seat taken?"

"Nope," I mumbled.

Kerry sat down next to me, pulled off his Tevas, and dipped his feet in the water beside mine.

"Nice feet," I said. I couldn't bring myself to look Kerry in the eye.

"Those long second toes of ours should have tipped us off."

I sighed. "What a mess."

"Yeah."

We skipped pebbles across the lake for a few minutes. "You know, I've been thinking," Kerry said. "Maybe, realistically, what happened is for the best."

What? "How's that?"

"Chances aren't great that we'd have lasted long as boyfriend-girlfriend."

What?

"But now we're relatives," Kerry continued. "Stuck together for life. Ten years from now, we may even laugh about this." He didn't look convinced.

"It's not just about *us*, Kerry," I spat. "For sixteen years, I believed that Mike was my real father. Now, I'm an orphan."

Kerry startled me by laughing out loud. "Charlie-girl, there's a guy I met up at the house. He *looks* like a father.

Talks like a father. He even shook my hand. There I was, thinking he'd rip my head off for messing with you—and *he shakes my hand.* He's okay, Charlie. And he looks straight as a pin. Like he'd never show up drunk for church, or stoned at a village meeting, or make a pass at your homeroom teacher . . . . Or run cocaine."

"Mike drinks beer," I said, defensively. He wasn't a total Mr. Rogers.

Kerry smirked. "To excess?"

"Not since the Senators lost the Eastern Conference."

"Does he smoke?"

"No. But he told me he once ate a hash brownie at university."

Kerry grinned. "Well, pardon me. He does live on the edge. Maybe your dad could adopt me, too."

"You're too old to be adopted. Besides, you still have a mother."

"I'd be less screwed up if I'd been raised by wolves. Besides, you haven't heard?"

"Heard what?"

"Mom packed up the Corolla and left last night, less than an hour after your Grams spilled the beans. She's gone for good. Says she's sick of being the laughingstock of Lake Ringrose. Went to stay with Lisa. She's putting the house and store up for sale. I'm sure more than a few villagers are already planning a 'good riddance' celebration."

"You're *moving?*" I was aghast.

"No way. Lake Ringrose is my home whether my so-called 'family' is here or not. I talked to Doc Will last night. If I do my share of cleaning and repairs, I can stay on his fold-out couch until I've finished school and saved enough money to

Trist

build on the back lot. And I'm pretty sure Tom Billings—he owns the marina—will let me keep my boat there in exchange for helping him with the winter maintenance."

"Kerry?"

"Mmm?"

"Does it gross you out? What we did?"

Kerry groaned. "We didn't know, Charlie-girl. Is it still incest if you don't know? I don't know. It was just . . . well, you know what it was."

I cringed. "Imagine if we'd slept together?"

Kerry picked at a splinter in the dock. "Truthfully, I 'imagined' it lots of times—before yesterday. And if you were honest, you'd admit you imagined it, too. Does the thought of us having sex gross me out now? I don't know. Probably. It's definitely not cool to date your sister, even out here in the sticks. *But we didn't know.*"

"Maybe we should have figured it out on our own," I said.

"Or maybe Josie or my mother should have been straight about it from the get-go. But we can't go back and erase what happened this summer. Besides, there are worse crimes than falling head over heels in love with someone you *don't know* is your half-sibling. Take it from me, your big brother Kerry, the one with the rap sheet."

We watched the clouds for a few minutes. "I guess it's the end of us competing in the Four Islands Race," I said finally.

"No!"

"But everything's different now. It's weird between us."

"It doesn't have to be. Not everything."

"You're handling all of this rather well," I said sarcastically.

"Trust me, Charlie-girl, I wasn't," Kerry said. "Last night, once I knew you were okay, I was seriously pissed off and raced out to the treehouse; I'm still surprised I didn't hit a tree. All I kept thinking was how *nothing* ever works out for me the way I want it to. How everything I do ends up screwy or ruined. But at the same time, I couldn't get it out of my head that you were—*are*—the best friend I've ever had. And we go like hell in a canoe. So I say we make a pact."

"Okay," I agreed warily.

"From now on we keep our hands and lips to ourselves, but nothing else changes. I lost Lisa to the city. I lost my father to the lake. I don't want to lose you to embarrassment—or whatever it is that's keeping you from looking me in the eye."

I glanced at up at Kerry. "Aren't you mad about Geri cheating with your dad?" I asked.

"Maybe if my mother was Carol Brady. But face it, Charlie-girl, you're living proof that out of two people's mutual stupidity can come something beautiful."

"You think I'm beautiful?" Now he tells me.

"Sure. Except when you scowl at me like that," he laughed. "Then you look like a hag."

A strange sound escaped my throat, part laugh, part sob. "I still love you, Kerry," I said. Maybe I loved him even more now that he was my brother.

His voice was husky. "I still love you, too." A long pause. "So, are we still on for the race?"

"Yeah. Okay. Sure."

Another long pause.

Kerry suddenly leapt up on the dock and pointed towards the water with alarm. "Look! An eel!"

I jumped up, ready to bolt.

"You're so gullible." Kerry laughed, and hip-checked me into the lake. He dove in after me and we raced out fifty meters from shore, splashed around, then raced back when we saw Grams and Mike dragging lawn chairs, coffee mugs, and citronella candles down to the dock. Kerry and I dried off and for the next hour, the four of us sat together and talked about easy stuff: hockey, cars, music. Anyone passing by might have seen us as we were.

A family.

Chapter Twenty-Six

Four Islands Race day dawned foggy and unseasonably cool.

"Don't fret about the weather," Grams said when she caught me frowning out the window. "The fog will burn off by race time."

Kerry and I had hauled Grams' canoe to the village wharf the previous afternoon. The competing pairs, all twelve of us, would begin there at ten-minute intervals. Kerry and I were in eighth position. In the end, it would be race times that mattered, not which team finished first. And though Kerry and I were competing just for fun, I'd been secretly entertaining fantasies of victory.

Kerry roared up Grams' lane on the ATV just in time for her to load us up with scrambled eggs and heaping bowls of apple-raisin oatmeal.

"Hey, you. Nervous?" Kerry asked me, then plunked down at the kitchen table and began shoveling in the food in like a bulldozer.

"Terrified."

"Good. Nothing like a shot of adrenaline to get your muscles working overtime."

"Aren't *you* nervous?" I asked.

Kerry put down his spoon and took a long drink of freshly-squeezed grapefruit juice. His face puckered. "For different reasons."

"What do you mean?"

"Nothing, hopefully."

"I don't understand."

But maybe I did. Not once during our canoe training or when I'd accompanied him on delivery trips in his outboard had Kerry ventured straight out into the middle of the lake.

Twenty minutes later, Kerry and I were headed for the village. Grams waved us off, wished us well, and promised to be at the finish line with her camera by early afternoon.

I was expecting Mike at the finish line, too. He'd returned to Toronto three days after my world shifted, to finish marking his Accounting finals and move his belongings back to Springdale. It had only been ten days since I'd seen him, but I was anxiously awaiting his return. I'd miss Grams and Kerry and the great outdoors like crazy, but it was time for me to go home. Back to Springdale. With my dad.

Race check-in time was nine-thirty, with Team One scheduled for take-off at ten sharp.

"If anyone gives you weird looks, ignore them," Kerry warned me as he parked the ATV and stashed our helmets in the cargo hold.

"I've been getting weird looks all my life."

"It's just . . . my mother didn't leave town quietly. And most of the village kids are home now from their camps and park jobs. Gossip spreads faster than poison ivy in these parts."

We did get a few stares and comments as we walked through the village, mostly from Kerry's peers, many of whom had recently arrived home from their summer jobs and made it their first order of business to be briefed on the latest village rumors.

A girl about my age fell into step beside us. She pointed at me. "Who's this, Kerry?" It was obvious from her catty expression that she already knew. I watched her gaze shifting from Kerry to me, then back to Kerry, looking for physical similarities.

"Kellie, this is Charlie, my half-sister." Kerry and I agreed there was no point trying to dispel rumors. After all, one day I'd be a regular part of the Lake Ringrose community; it was best to get the truth out now, get the awkwardness over with. And as far as Kerry knew, the community at large only knew about Greg Sanderson fathering Geri Parsons' daughter, not about Kerry and I making out in the woods. I was thankful that those who knew about *that* were keeping their mouths shut.

"Does Lisa know?" piped an older guy standing nearby.

"Lisa knows everything," Kerry replied with an air of confidence I knew he didn't feel. Lisa hadn't called. But then, he mused, it would take more than the discovery of a long lost sister to faze Lisa. "She probably just shrugged and made some scathing remark to Mom about the likelihood of us having half-siblings all over Northern Ontario. Cripes, you think?"

"Team Eight!" called a man with a megaphone. "On your mark!"

"That's us!" I waved.

"Good luck!" a few kids yelled as Kerry and I rushed to the wharf.

"Break a leg!" someone else shouted.

"Been there, done that!" Kerry yelled back.

"You're looking good, Kerry," said a blonde in a tangerine bikini. She'd been trailing us along the wharf, waiting for an opportunity to say her piece.

"Thanks, Gina," Kerry replied, brushing her off.

"Will I see you at the dance tonight?" she asked.

"I'll be there," he said, and kept walking.

Gina pouted and slunk back to the horde of teens from Wawa who'd come to Lake Ringrose on a school bus to watch the race.

"Gina was my girlfriend," he explained. "The one who broke up with me after my injury. The one who thought I'd be in a wheelchair the rest of my life. The one who couldn't stomach having a boyfriend with a catheter bag hanging from his hospital bed."

"Sounds like she's changed her mind about you."

"Jealous?" I couldn't tell if he was making a joke or not.

"Absolutely not," I lied. Truth was, I had no idea what I felt for Kerry anymore. The transition from boyfriend to brother seemed smooth enough on the outside, but inside I was still a mess of awkward feelings. I wondered if it was the same for Kerry. He kept his hands in his pockets a lot when he was with me now, like he didn't know what to do with them if he couldn't touch me.

"TEAM EIGHT! ARE YOU READY OR NOT?" Megaphone-man bellowed.

Without another word, Kerry and I slid Grams' canoe into the water. I untied the painter and took my position in the bow. Kerry waited for the starting pistol with one foot on the wharf and the other in the stern.

BANG!

I gave a war whoop and Kerry pushed us off the wharf amid shouts of encouragement from the crowd. We took up our paddles, found our rhythm quickly, and we stroked, stroked, stroked towards Island One, nearly a kilometer away.

"Don't get frantic, Charlie-girl," Kerry called up to me. "Nice and steady wins the race. It's like that story about the rabbit and the turtle."

"You mean 'The Tortoise and the Hare'?"

"Whatever. All I'm saying is don't spend all your energy now; we don't know what the challenges will be."

Despite nice and steady paddling, we still managed to arrive at Island One ahead of Team Seven. Once on land, Kerry and I were given a long strip of cloth and were instructed to tie my left leg to Kerry's right. Our challenge was to run a three-legged lap around a hundred-meter course marked with orange tape.

Not our best event. Kerry was taller than me by a good six inches. We kept stumbling over each other's feet on the hills and turns.

"Are you okay?" I kept asking. I worried that Kerry would trip the wrong way and pop a femur.

"I'm fine, dammit," Kerry said as we lurched around the last pylon. "I'm not made of glass, you know."

We made it back to the canoe just seconds before Team Seven caught up.

"Forget slow and steady for now!" Kerry shouted, tossing me my life vest and paddle. "We've got to stay ahead of them!"

More paddling. Kerry and I were pumped, our frantic pace making up for time lost during the three-legged race. We pulled up to the Island Two dock just minutes behind Team Six.

The second challenge was an obstacle relay. We were dead meat.

"Go first." Kerry shoved me forward, gently, but leaving no space for argument; the clock was ticking.

"Okay, okay." I climbed up and over a steep A-frame, hopped through a row of tires, crawled under a long tarp strung just eighteen inches off the ground. Now I knew what Jack Russell dogs felt like at agility competitions. I *almost* made it over the shallow bog using a rope swing; instead, I fell face first into a foot of barf-green slime. Kerry laughed his guts out. You'll get yours, I thought, spouting a mouthful of mud in his general direction.

And he did. Kerry made it fine over the A-frame, through the tires, and under the tarp. He bellowed like Tarzan as he cleared the bog with two feet to spare. But he tripped over a rock along the final straightaway and landed in a pile of brush. A nasty inch-long splinter had to be extracted from his palm by the first-aid-kit-wielding race official before Kerry was cleared to continue. By the time we left for Island Three, Team Seven had passed us and Team Nine was closing in.

Once again, Kerry and I were sleek on the water and easily regained our position ahead of Team Seven.

The Island Three challenge was a scavenger hunt. Kerry's knowledge of the Lake Ringrose woods was a real asset. We had to collect a maple leaf; he knew there was just one maple on the island *and* where it was. We had to find a piece of rose quartz; while Team Six frantically searched in vain along the wooded island trail, Kerry led me along the shore to a tiny secluded beach littered with the pink stuff.

Back in the canoe, Kerry and I trailed Team Five. We were nowhere near first place time-wise, but Kerry was confident we'd make the top five as long as our paddling stayed strong.

As we neared the center of the lake, the wind shifted. Kerry and I had to pull like oxen to keep pace. My shoulders throbbed underneath my life vest but I'd let my arms fall off into the lake before I'd suggest to Kerry that I needed a break.

About two hundred meters from Island Four, he suddenly dug his paddle deep into the water and pulled back.

"What are you doing!" I yelled over my shoulder.

"Watch out for the rock."

Sure enough, there was a rock just to the right of us, a *huge* rock, its rounded peak submerged just a few inches below the lake's surface.

"The water's high this summer," Kerry said in the same flat voice. "Usually, this rock juts a foot or two above the lake surface by Labour Day."

"Thanks for the geography lesson." I attempted to resume our pace, but Kerry negated my efforts by sweeping his paddle and drawing us closer to the rock's edge. Before I had a chance to object, he stood up. The canoe lurched. Grabbing the painter for leverage, Kerry shakily stepped out of the canoe and onto the rock. The water lapped around his feet and ankles.

"What the hell!" I yelled. "Are we in a race or not?"

"This is the rock," Kerry said.

Oh.

The rock. The rock he'd been avoiding all summer. The rock responsible for the web of scars on Kerry's legs. The rock where his dad, *my* drug-running biological father, died trying to elude the cops. The rock, Kerry once admitted, that still gave him nightmares.

grist

Team Six caught up to us and shot us odd looks. "Everything okay?" the guy, a gray-haired summer cottager, asked.

Kerry waved them past. "We'll catch up."

"You wish," his wife laughed as they sailed past.

I held out my hand to Kerry. He pulled me out of the canoe. We just stood there on the rock awhile not saying a word. My thoughts were spinning, so I could only imagine what was going on in *Kerry's* mind. When he shifted his weight and lost his balance, he fell backwards into the water with barely a splash. Kerry surfaced, inhaled deeply, and stared up at the deep blue sky. He looked like he might shout something, but he didn't.

Another team was approaching.

"Kerry?" I said. "You want to bow out? It's okay by me."

He shook water from his hair. "No way. Let's finish this for the old man. Let's kick some serious ass. Let's show the stupid bastard that his long-toed offspring aren't out of the race."

"Kerry?"

"Yeah."

I gestured to the sky. "You think Geri and Greg are up there together in the cheap seats cheering us on?"

He wiped his nose on his arm and grinned. "Wanna moon them?"

"Nah. Let's just make them proud."

Kerry and I dove back into the canoe. Fueled by sheer determination and the dregs of Grams' high-octane oatmeal, we raced towards Island Four as if powered by a forty horse-power engine.

"What are you crazy kids up to?" Team Six wanted to know as we landed at the Island Four dock neck and neck with them.

Kerry laughed. "Beating the pants off you."

The Island Four challenge was a swim relay. Each participant had to complete one lap around the circumference of the island, about three hundred meters.

Team Six groaned; the man was a poor swimmer and would need to make his lap wearing a life vest. And Team Five, the race official informed us, had been forced to drop out when the female participant suffered an asthma attack. Not to be insensitive, but Kerry and I were in luck.

"Ladies first." Kerry gestured for me to take the first lap.

"If this race doesn't paralyze my upper body, I'll be able to arm wrestle gorillas when I get back to Springdale," I complained, quickly chucking my life vest.

Kerry massaged my shoulders. "Charlie-girl, if we can stay ahead of Team Six and somehow wedge ourselves between Teams Three and Four, we could win this thing. Give it your all!"

He was lying about us being able to win—the formidable Team Eleven, comprised of the perennial champs from Thunder Bay, was already on our tail—but Kerry knew I was aching and needed a boost of false hope to keep my muscles from going on strike. As he rubbed my arms, a familiar current ran up my spine and gave me goosebumps. Kerry stopped abruptly; he felt it, too. How long would it be before we could touch each other like siblings? Did siblings touch each other at all?

Kerry stepped back. "Get in that water! And no doggie-paddling!"

I dove into the lake with all the grace of a baby hippo. Spotters were sprinkled around the island shouting encouragement and clutching life-saving equipment that I hoped I wouldn't need.

"Pace yourself!" Kerry shouted.

Ten minutes into the lap, my arms were like dead weights, but I sucked it up and swam like I had Jaws on my tail. I heard a whoop of glee that could have only been Kerry as I splashed quickly past the fatigued Team Four swimmer who'd resorted to an awkward sidestroke. Despite my speed, I flinched each time my legs brushed against the slimy underwater foliage; I'd never really lost my fear of lake monsters.

My lap completed, Kerry yanked me up onto the dock, wrapped me up like a burrito in a beach towel, and was in the water himself within seconds. The break he'd had while I swam my lap had served him well; he cut through the water like a dolphin.

Only nineteen minutes after setting out, Kerry and the Team Four swimmer I'd passed arrived at the dock chatting between strokes about hockey.

"Charlie, this is Kevin," Kerry said as he quickly toweled himself off and re-donned his life vest.

"Nice to meet—" I started.

Kerry tossed me my paddle. "Save the formalities for later. Let's roll."

"Team Eleven's going to win again this year," Kerry admitted as they grunted brusquely and sailed past us. "Their time is phenomenal this year. Kevin told me that the woman used to be a world-class kayak champion and the guy completed an eco-challenge in South America last winter. We might as well give up."

I fought the urge to turn around and whomp Kerry over the head with my paddle. "What!" I yelled over my shoulder.

He grinned. "Just kidding. My time with Lisa last summer was three hours, seven minutes and sixteen seconds." He checked his sports watch. "That gives us thirty-three minutes to get to shore if we want to beat last year's time."

"Can we make it?" I surveyed the village in the distance.

"Easily."

"Maybe if we keep training on our own over the winter, we can win next summer. Or at least give Team Eleven a better run for their money."

"You'll be back next summer? For sure?"

I nodded. I couldn't imagine what it would take to keep me away from Lake Ringrose. But I also knew how many things could change in a year. "You'll probably have trained yourself another female partner by next summer."

Kerry put down his paddle. "Charlie-girl, let's make another pact. No matter what happens to us during the rest of the year, the Four Islands Race will always be a family thing. *Our* thing."

Something to look forward to. "Deal," I agreed.

Kerry resumed his paddling position. "Good. Now let's just shut up and stroke!"

Chapter Twenty-Seven

Kerry and I sailed under the finish banner and onto the village beach amid cheers from a humongous crowd. We'd barely, but gloriously, nabbed third place! Everyone from the village had turned out, and from the looks of it, so had most of Wawa and the surrounding resorts. Little kids waved from the wharf, balloons tied to their wrists and ice cream dripping down their chins. I saw Grams and the Doc perched on a large piece of driftwood on the beach. Doc Will had his arm around Grams, beaming like it was he who'd won a prize. I may not have a stepmother any time soon, but it looked like I might have a step-grandfather by next summer.

I could live with that.

I scanned the shore and noticed Mike's van parked in front of the post office. I was happy he'd made it in time for the finish.

Kerry spotted him first. "Who's that with Mike?" he asked.
"Where?"

"Over there." He pointed. "Far edge of the wharf. Looks like the Jolly Green Giant."

"What the . . . ?"

No way.

"AAAAAHHHHHHHHH!" I yelled, vaulting out of the canoe and ripping off my life vest, my fatigue obliterated. I ran full speed along the beach, up the creaky wooden stairs, and along the wharf. I plowed into Sam's ratty, emerald, Springdale Sonics' T-shirt with such force that I knocked him clean off his feet. We both landed in the water and came up sputtering.

"WHAT THE HELL ARE YOU DOING HERE!" I screamed before Sam even had time to shake the water from his nose.

"It's a long story."

Fine with me. I could tread water all afternoon if I had to.

Turned out Sam's father *had* accepted a year-long extension of his Australian post. After that, he was eligible for early retirement and planned to take it. Mr. Garrison wanted to come back to Springdale and spend the rest of his life playing golf and lounging by the pool.

"So what is this? A vacation?" Just being with Sam again for a few minutes seemed too good to be true. I wondered if he was a mirage. Maybe I had sunstroke.

Sam shook his head. "I'm back to stay. I'll live with Aunt Carol for the school year. My parents want me to finish the computer program at Springdale High before I decide what to do about my future. Mom says my brain may be ready for the 'uni' but that the rest of me isn't. And well . . . I missed *you,* Charlie."

Hemissedmehemissedmehemissedme . . . *YES!*

"Won't you miss your family?" I asked.

"Nah. I get to fly back at Christmas for two weeks. The government will pay for me and one escort. Want to go to Australia in December?"

That was *way* too much information for me to digest at once. I wanted to say something meaningful to Sam, something coherent even, but my head was still reeling. I grinned like an idiot. "When did you get back to Canada?"

"Three days ago," Sam explained. "I was biking around and spotted Mike unloading stuff from his van. He invited me to come with him to pick you up this weekend. I wasn't sure if it was such a good idea, but—"

"Why wouldn't it have been a good idea?"

"Well, with you and Kerry and . . ." Sam blushed.

"Mike told you, didn't he?" I asked accusingly. "About what happened? About Kerry being my brother?"

"Well . . . yeah. It was a long ride up here. I think Mike thought it was best if I knew what was going on. So I wouldn't say something unbelievably stupid to you."

"You can laugh if you want to. I know you're dying to."

"Well, at least you won't be able to tease me about Madame Dumas anymore," Sam snickered, splashing me.

I splashed him back.

Then he dunked me.

I grappled for Sam's legs under the water and pulled his leg hair—hard.

Sam yelped.

It was like old times.

When our lips turned blue and our teeth chattered, Sam and I hoisted ourselves onto the wharf.

"Cripes, Charlie, you've got bigger triceps than me," he exclaimed.

"That's not saying much." I felt self-conscious standing there in my dripping bathing suit; I felt Sam's eyes on me, and not just on my triceps, either.

Mike walked over and I gave him a sopping hug. "Thank you," I whispered in his ear.

He beamed. "My pleasure. I knew you'd be surprised. And pleased. Let me get us all some drinks." He joined the long line at the snack bar. Jenny's Café was boarded up. Stupid, I thought. She could have made a killing that afternoon.

On the beach, a slim, dark-haired girl strode over to where Kerry was talking to Grams and Doc Will. She gave Kerry an enthusiastic hug. Another old girlfriend? It wouldn't take Kerry long to get over me, that was for sure.

But wait. The pair disengaged quickly and headed towards Sam and me. Kerry was jaunty with excitement. The girl kept pace.

As they got closer, I realized that I knew the girl. We'd never met, but I recognized the way she cocked her head at me appraisingly. The arch of her eyebrows. Something about her stride.

"Hi, Lisa," I said.

Lisa smirked back. "Welcome to the Addams Family." Her attention turned to Sam in his droopy shorts and dripping green T-shirt. He had a long slimy strand of lake foliage stuck in his hair. "You Swamp Boy?"

"G'day. I'm Sam," he said with a fake Aussie accent. Once a dork, always a dork.

"Hey." Kerry shook his hand and tossed me the towel I'd left in the canoe. I rubbed my hair with it then passed the towel to Sam like a reflex. He and I'd been sharing things our whole lives: our toys, our Slurpees, our swim towels. It had only been the important things we'd kept to ourselves.

Kerry glanced back at the crowd. "Mom with you?" he asked Lisa.

Lisa shook her head. "I came alone. Just wanted to see this Charlie-sister before she went back to wherever she's been all these years. And to get my leftover stuff out of the house before Mom sells it." She rummaged through her purse for cigarettes and lit up. After a long drag, she offered the cigarette to Kerry, who waved it off.

"When did you start smoking?" he asked.

Lisa took another drag. "Same day Mom invited herself to live with me. It's just until she finds an apartment."

"I'm sorry that my being here this summer opened up such a slimy barrel of worms," I said.

Kerry shook his head. "It's not your fault. If not you, then someone or something else would have set her off eventually. Mom's been a minefield since Lisa and I were little kids."

Lisa nodded. "Honestly, Charlie, I think it was all for the best. Mom's happier now than I've ever seen her. And more open. Yesterday she told me something that I've always known; that some people—meaning her and me—aren't cut out for lives surrounded by hills and forests and water."

Kerry mumbled, "Whatever," and turned his attention to a luxury houseboat that had pulled up to the wharf.

"Mom actually praised me for being sensible when I used university to leave," Lisa continued. "She admitted taking off to New York City when she was eighteen to be a dancer had been a huge mistake, but that returning to Lake Ringrose and 'settling' had been an even bigger one. She's got her eye on a vacant house near campus. She thinks she might be able to convert the upper level into an apartment for herself and re-open Jenny's Café on the ground floor." Lisa glanced over at Kerry, whose attention was still focused on the houseboat; he was pointing out to Sam the on-board electronic equipment and below-deck sleeping compartments. She lowered her voice. "Kerry might not know it yet, but he's much better off on his own, now, too.

"Trust me, he knows it."

Kerry and Sam re-joined the conversation. "The dance starts at eight," Kerry said. He raised a eyebrow at me. "You're staying, right?"

I nodded. Mike had no intention of driving back to Springdale until the next morning.

Lisa crushed out her cigarette with the heel of her sandal. She had long second toes, too. "What's the theme this year?"

"Music and Movies of the Eighties," I replied. "There'll be a best costume prize and an air band contest."

Lisa snorted. "I'll come as Madonna." She thrust her hips around the wharf. *"Like a virgin . . ."* She stopped suddenly. "Who will you be emulating, Kerwin?"

"What the hell kind of word is *emulating?* I'm *going* as Tom Cruise in *Top Gun.* Doc Will's going to lend me his old flight jacket and goggles."

"Why not go as Tom Cruise in *Risky Business* instead?" Lisa asked. "You'd just have to show up in your underwear."

"Because my legs aren't Tom Cruise material."

"You think your face is?"

"Love you, too, Lisa."

Lisa turned and looked me over.

I shook out my wind-blown, sun-bleached hair. "What do you think? Cindy Lauper?"

"Girls just want to have fu-un . . ." Lisa sang in off-key falsetto. "Sure. I can see it." Then she turned to Sam. "What about you?"

"What?" he asked, suddenly self-conscious.

"You, mate," Kerry said, pointing. "Crocodile Dundee."

Chapter Twenty-Eight

After the dance, Sam, Lisa and I traveled in Lisa's car to the back lot trail where we met up with Kerry on his ATV. We hiked with flashlights through the chilly early-September night to the tree house. Lisa was agile and fearless in the forest despite her self-proclaimed assimilation to city life.

I knew Sam felt out of place, in the way, *overwhelmed* just to be back in Canada. He'd taken me aside right after the dance to say he'd stay behind at Grams' so I could spend time alone with my half-siblings on my last night at Lake Ringrose. I told him not to be a goof and pulled him along through the dark forest. He flinched at every rustle of the bushes.

"Don't you guys ever hike back in Springdale?" Kerry asked him.

Sam smirked. "Only from home to the 7-Eleven for bags of Doritos."

"Can you believe Mike tonight?" I said once we'd all climbed up into the tree house. "I wish someone had taped it."

In a turn of events that both mortified and amazed me, Mike had arrived at the dance wearing tight Levis and an ancient Bruce Springsteen T-shirt that he'd borrowed from some guy he met at the marina. He then proceeded to wow the air band judges (we'd appointed the victorious Team Eleven to do the honors) bringing down the house—or *wharf* as it was—with "Dancing In The Dark." "I bet if Barb had seen that side of him, they'd still be together," I said to Sam.

Sam guffawed. "Who knew old Mike had it in him."

"I don't know what came over me," Mike laughed earlier, after he accepted his prize—a monstrous, beer-filled cooler shaped like a lake trout. "The fresh air must have gone to my head."

Mike knew I'd be spending the night at the treehouse. And I knew he'd be sleeping in the hammock on Grams' porch like he had the first time he'd come. Sleeping in Geri's old room wasn't an option for either of us anymore; boxes were piled everywhere. Grams had skipped the dance; her ("he is not!") date, the Doc, had been called away to deliver a baby. Instead, she spent the evening packing up my mother's old books—and the sketchbook—for me to take home to Springdale, and sorting other items to be donated to the next village rummage sale. Grams planned to renovate. To turn the space into a guest room. To take in a boarder.

"A boarder named Kerry?" I'd asked.

Grams grinned. "I know Will offered him his couch, but I want to give Kerry a real room here. I want to make sure he eats properly. Hardworking men shouldn't live on Coke and granola bars."

Kerry, Lisa, Sam, and I spent the night awake, talking, laughing, and scarfing everything in the food cache. Kerry played nostalgic folk tunes on his guitar for a while. Lisa told Sam and me some native stories she'd picked up from Cree and Ojibway schoolmates over the years, and about the rock paintings, called "pictographs," of the hairy, prankish "river fairies" at nearby Missinabi Lake. Sam taught us a new Australian curse word every time he banged his head on the tree house rafters. I sat back and took it all in.

"How did you get the scars on your nose?" Kerry asked Sam at one point. Sam had burned his face in the sun and four tiny lines stood out white against the red.

"He got scratched by a cat," I piped up.

"They look like bite marks to me," Kerry remarked, grinning.

Sam told Kerry the truth. "When we were five years old, I *accidentally* ripped the cover off one of Charlie's Franklin books."

"Accident, my ass," I sneered.

"Charlie chased me all over the house and pinned me down on the kitchen floor—she was bigger than me back then. She bit my nose and wouldn't let go until I promised to give her my *101 Dalmations* video as compensation."

Kerry leaned over in hysterics. "I think, Sam, that she was flirting with you."

At the crack of dawn, a crystal clear dawn so cold we could see our breath, Lisa recruited Sam to go back to the A-frame with her to help load boxes of personal items into her car. She wanted to make it down to Sudbury by early afternoon. Her plan was to crash at her boyfriend's dorm for a few days and let Jenny think she was still at Lake Ringrose.

"More than twenty-four hours here at a stretch makes Lisa break out in hives," Kerry explained.

Lisa promised to drop Sam off at Grams' by eight-thirty. Kerry and I would clean the garbage out of the tree house, then take the ATV back to the village in time to hook up with Mike, Sam, and Grams for breakfast and goodbyes.

Lisa had pulled me aside when Kerry disappeared to check his minnow traps. "Kerry was such a mess after what happened last winter, Charlie; you have no idea. But he'll be okay now. You've been there for Kerry this summer in a way that I never was."

I blushed purple.

Lisa groaned. "That's *not* what I meant," she said. "It's just . . . well . . . I've always been so full of practical, 'big-sisterly' advice for Kerry, based mostly on what works for me. But advice isn't what he needs. Just hearing him talk so excitedly last night about that cottage he still wants to build here some-day—it made me realize that Kerry totally knows what he wants to do with his life, maybe even more than I do. You and Dad are the only ones who ever respected his choice to stay here at the lake, to make a life here. Who weren't out to change him. I hope you and I will stay in touch."

"Me, too," I replied.

"Oh, and just so you know, your dad's hot," she added, laughing.

"Mike? He's available, if you don't mind dating your half-sister's adoptive father."

Lisa cringed. "Too messy for me. But hey, Kangaroo Boy's not bad, either."

I glanced over at Sam. He was pretending to tie his sneakers, but I could tell by his crimson ears that he'd been listening.

"You're in luck," I said, not caring. "He likes older women."

Lisa bent over and whispered in my ear. "I'm taken. Besides, the way he was looking at you last night, I'd say Sam's tastes may be changing."

No, they weren't. I was older, too. By a whopping two weeks.

After Lisa and Sam left, Kerry plunked down next to where I was sitting on the air bed. "Hey, you."

I blinked away a flashback to the last time Kerry and I were alone on the air bed. "I'm going to miss you," I said.

"You won't miss me at all," Kerry scoffed.

Wouldn't he miss *me?*

"Don't think you can get rid of me just by going home to Springdale," he said. "I'll be down to visit with your Grams at Thanksgiving. And don't be surprised if I call you every damn night for help with my English homework."

"I'll miss you anyway," I said, rising to sweep stray leaves and granola bar crumbs through the floor cracks.

Kerry got up, too, and headed for the floor hatch. "Way too much Coke last night. Be right back."

Not five minutes later, I smelled Kerry coming up the ladder before I saw him, though at the time I didn't realize it was him. I smelled something familiar, something that sparked a deeply rooted memory—*but not one of Kerry.* I sucked in my breath and quickly turned from where I was now dusting cobwebs from the rafters.

Of course it was Kerry. Who else could it have been? But the sight of him made me chew my lip like crazy, made me blink back a sudden swell of tears. I was numb, not with shock, but with stupid realization. I should have known.

"Hey, you," he said again.

"Kerry? Where did you get that leather jacket?" I choked out.

"It was in the tool shed by the pond."

"No, no, no. That's not what I meant. That jacket isn't yours. It's *old.* Who did you get it from? Why haven't I seen you wear it before today?"

"I haven't needed it before today. Why are you so upset?"

I turned to the window and stifled a sob. "Did your father, did Greg, did he make . . . carvings?"

Kerry shrugged. "Yeah. He was always whittling away at something: wood, limestone, soap. He was pretty good at it, even won a few ribbons at fairs and exhibitions. As for me," he added, "when I'm working with my hands, I'd rather it be at something practical, like building a dock, or—"

"Did he ever carve chocolate?"

"Charlie, why are you crying?"

"Answer the goddam question!" I demanded. *"Please.* Did he ever carve chocolate?"

"Sure. When Lisa and I were small, Dad would carve wild animals out of chocolate for Christmas and birthdays and whatever. Why are you freaking? You're scaring me."

I ignored Kerry question and asked another of my own. "Did he have a skull ring?"

"He used to, years ago, until he got frostbite on his fingers one winter. The ring didn't fit him anymore. I don't know what happened to it. It was just a piece of junk."

I'd heard enough. "He was the Chocolate Moose Man," I whispered.

"Charlie-girl, I don't know what you're talking about."

I looked deep into his eyes and tried to keep my voice steady. "He was . . . I met him. Your . . . our . . . Greg. He came to my mother's funeral. I remember the jacket and the ring. And he gave me a moose carved of chocolate."

The man with the tough-guy clothes and the gentle eyes had been my biological father. I absolutely knew then what Kerry had been telling me all summer was true; Greg Sanderson was more than a second-rate husband, bad-example parent, and criminal. He'd come to see me when my mother died—despite the scandal it may have caused—to pay his respects and to make sure that I was okay. He didn't confront Mike or Grams, or cause a scene, or try to pull me into an embrace that might have terrified me. He just came in and sat down beside me on a bench out in the church foyer where I'd gone to escape the crying adults and said . . .

"You're so pretty. Just like your mother."

"My mommy died," I replied. I wasn't sure what that meant, just that she was gone to a place called Heaven and wasn't ever coming back.

"Are you sad?" he asked.

I nodded. "My daddy Mike is sad, too."

"Your daddy loved your mommy very much," the Moose Man said.

I brightened. "He said that tomorrow we can go to the park and get some ice cream. Mommy's favorite is chocolate."

The Moose Man grinned then, that same grin he'd passed on to his son. The grin I'd mistakenly confused with Brad Pitt's. "Do you like chocolate, too?" he asked.

I giggled a little. Didn't everyone?

He reached into his leather jacket pocket, pulled out the cellophane-covered moose and handed it to me. I noticed the scary skull ring then, but it was quickly overshadowed by the moose. "That's a funny horse," I said, examining the little chocolate creature.

"It's a moose."

"A moose," I repeated. I was pretty sure that there weren't any moose in Springdale.

"Moose live in the forest where your mommy and I grew up."

"Thank you for the moose," I said.

"You're welcome, Charlena. You have a pretty name."

"My mommy calls me Charlie."

"It's been nice meeting you, Charlie."

"Are you someone's daddy?" I asked.

The Moose Man nodded slowly. His warm eyes looked sad. "I have a little girl who's six. And a five-year-old boy."

"Can I play with them sometime?"

The Moose Man sighed. "I hope you'll all be friends one day."

I unwrapped the cellophane from the moose and chomped down on the antlers. "Yummy." I smiled, showing chocolate teeth. Then the sadness of the day overwhelmed me again and a tear slipped onto my cheek.

The Moose Man mussed my hair and said solemnly, "Don't cry, Charlie. Be tough like your mommy. Be strong for your daddy Mike."

And then he was gone.

Kerry engulfed me in the jacket now, held me tight for the first time since all hell broke loose. There were no fireworks now. No snap, crackle, or pop. No anger or sadness or regret. Just a much-needed calm.

"There's still so much I want to know about you," Kerry said into my hair.

If Greg Sanderson and my mother were still alive, they'd have a lot of explaining to do. Hard to believe that after ten very long weeks at Lake Ringrose, I still didn't have a clear picture of who my mother had been. And I knew even less about the Chocolate Moose Man. I guess if I'd learned about anyone that summer, it was about myself. Maybe that was what mattered most.

That and honoring my new responsibilities. I was a sibling now; I had a brother and sister to make proud and buy for at Christmas. I was an adoptee; I'd never take Mike for granted, or complain about his choice of pizza toppings, or begrudge him a social life again. I had a disgustingly high fitness level to maintain. I'd even made shaky peace with the Lake Ringrose wildlife and my writing ambitions.

I had a life to live up to.

I had a future to plan.

I had grist!

"We've got the rest of our lives to get to know each other," I said to Kerry. There would be graduations, house-warmings, weddings, babies, vacations, Four Island Races—and funerals, too. We'd see plenty of each other.

I was sure of it.

Chapter Twenty-Nine

Three days later, the afternoon of the first day of school, I was summoned to the office of Hector "Quadruple Bypass" Pollen, my soon to be—if I groveled sufficiently—twelfth-grade creative writing teacher.

"Hello, sir," I said from the doorway.

Mr. Pollen looked up at me and stared for a full five seconds. He beckoned me in. "Charles?" he asked.

Despite the late-summer humidity, wearing a sleeveless shirt with my jeans had been a bad idea. Guys in my homeroom had been offering to arm-wrestle me. The jock girls had cornered me in the cafeteria at lunch and tried to recruit me for volleyball. I'd written to Kerry during third period study hall suggesting he'd perhaps gone overboard with my weight training. Springdale wasn't prepared for Charlie the Gladiator. Or *I* wasn't, in any case. Though I might try the volleyball thing.

"What did you do this summer," Mr. Pollen continued. "Swim the English Channel?"

"Sure felt like it at times." Hopefully he'd know soon enough how I spent my summer vacation.

"You wanted to see me?" he asked.

"I want into your senior writing class."

Grist

"You should have worked out your class schedule during registration week."

True, being out of town was no excuse—course selection was done via touch-tone phone—but I'd missed my assigned window during all the Lake Ringrose hoopla. "I was having a family crisis that week," I said.

"Sorry," Mr. Pollen said. "The class is full."

My face fell. "Okay. Thanks anyway," I mumbled and turned to leave.

"Charles?"

I turned back.

"I was joking. There's always room for you in my class, if—"

"*If?*" Would there always be a catch?

"You want in or not?"

Did I? "Yes."

Mr. Pollen cleared his throat. "*If,* then, you—"

"Let me guess," I interrupted. "If I promise to listen to your criticisms objectively."

Mr. Pollen nodded. "I guarantee that when you produce what I know you are capable of, my praise will be just as generous."

"Okay." I'd learn to suck it up if it killed me.

"That's not all."

"Of course not," I said, trying not to laugh. Mr. Pollen would never change. And maybe I loved him for that; he was the only adult in my life who'd never lied to me. "I need to learn to question myself, right?" I asked. "And to question the world. Nothing—not this town, this school, my friends, my foes, my *life*—is mundane if I see it through the eyes of a writer. A wad of green gum stuck to the sidewalk can be fabulous inspiration if I just ask the right questions. Was the gum dropped by a boy freshening his breath for a first kiss? Was it thrown out a car window by a passing celebrity? What if the gum was poison?"

"Right." Mr. Pollen agreed. "Stories can be anywhere. Expect the unexpected. Arthur Schopenhauer once said, 'The business of the novelist is not to relate great events, but to make the small ones interesting.'"

I knew that now. I learned it the hard way.

Mr. Pollen took a long swig from a water bottle perched on his desk. "Finally, you must listen to your heart. I ignored mine for years—I fed it doughnuts and fried chicken even when I knew it needed flax seeds and oat bran—and look what happened. You know in your heart, Charles, if you're a writer. It's not a job you choose; it chooses you. It's alive."

"But like any animal," I grinned, "it must be fed—by my experience and my willingness to learn."

There it was, that big, booming belly laugh that I'd missed so much. "Exactly, Charles!"

"Sir, why do you call me Charles?"

"I once knew a dentist named—"

"No, Mr. Pollen. I don't want a punchline. I want an answer. Please."

"I've had heart disease for almost fourteen years."

"Uh huh." I was sorry and all, but what did that have to do with anything?

"By chance, I suppose, your mother was scheduled for chemotherapy on the same days I was scheduled for my monthly EKG. We got talking in the waiting room on several occasions. When Mike would drop her off at the hospital in the mornings, you'd be riding high on his shoulders, scabs on your knees, hair sticking out all over. When Geri was called for her treatment, he'd take you down to the cafeteria, and you'd come back later with ice cream all over yourself and a big, gooey kiss for your mother when she was done."

"How is your heart now?" I asked.

He shrugged. "Still ticking, though in a different time zone. But aren't you curious to know what my having heart disease has to do with me calling you Charles?"

I nodded once more. I was starting to feel like one of those bobbleheads people stick on their dashboards.

Mr. Pollen took another drink of water. "I know you don't remember, but Geri was so proud of you," he continued. "She didn't give a hoot that you laughed and sang out loud in the hospital waiting room, where protocol suggests people be silent and morose-looking. You gave me so many chuckles, even then. You were such a tomboy, always full of beans. One day, you elbowed your way into a truck game two older boys—they must have been seven or eight—were playing, and proceeded to commandeer the whole show. Your mother just turned to me and said, 'We should have named her Charles.' I knew you had-n't changed the minute you walked into my first writing class."

"The hair?" I asked. My bat's nest would be the bane of my existence for the rest of my life. Or maybe if I called her and acted civil, Barb would still join me for that makeover day at World of Women.

Mr. Pollen chucked. "It was the way you *challenged* me at every turn. Your *temper* when things didn't go your way. But you scared me this past spring. It was like your fire had burned out. Like you'd stopped caring."

"I had writer's block." And heartache. And apathy. And boredom.

Mr. Pollen shook his head. "You were afraid."

I hated to admit it, but he was right. Dead on. I'd been afraid. A total chickenshit. Afraid of the future. Afraid of being left behind. Afraid of my own shadow.

"But something happened to you this summer, Charles," Mr. Pollen continued. "You don't have to tell me about it; I can see it in your eyes—and your biceps. You're back. You went somewhere where you learned to let yourself become a strong and lovely young woman. You came into your own without giving away the gifts your mother left you: her tenacity, her humor, her creativity."

"And her fallibility," I groaned. "Don't forget her fallibility." Like he even knew the half of it.

Mr. Pollen grinned. He'd cut back his beard and I could actually see his lips. He had a nice smile. "That, Charlena, is why I've always called you 'Charles'. It certainly was never intended as an insult, though I know you've outgrown the tomboy label. It was simply to remember the good-natured spirit of my friend Geri the last day I ever saw her." Mr. Pollen cleared his throat. "The writing class is in Room 306, third period." He glanced at the rest of my schedule. "You'll have to give up your study hall."

"That's fine." I'd give up my Saturdays if I had to, but he didn't need to know that.

"You missed today's class assignment," Mr. Pollen added, rifling through the papers on his desk for an extra copy.

"May I submit this instead?" I asked, pulling a thick wad of papers from my backpack.

Mr. Pollen stopped rummaging. "What's that? A novel?"

I passed the papers to him without comment. It had taken me until four in the morning to merge the original (pathetic)

Chocolate Moose Man Mystery with my summer journal. To distort timelines and skew facts. To sensationalize the mundane and anonymize (was that a word?) the main characters until it read more like a bizarre fantasy/strange nightmare than an autobiography.

Mr. Pollen grinned. "I'd been planning to read *War and Peace* tonight. I'll give this a go instead."

"Thanks, sir."

Mr. Pollen peered over my shoulder at someone lurking in the doorway.

Sam waved at him. "Sorry for interrupting. I'll be at your locker," he said to me and quickly disappeared.

Mr. Pollen walked me to the door. "May I assume that the tale of Charles and Sam has ended happily ever after?"

I recognized a trick question when I heard one. "The story's not over, Mr. Pollen. Not by a long shot. Who knows what grist is waiting for us all around the next corner?"

Heather Waldorf is a counselor at a North York group home for adults with developmental disabilities. She earned her B.A. in fine arts studies at York University and her B.Ed. in adult education at Brock. She wrote *Grist* during a coast-to-coast camping trip. This is her second YA novel, after *Fighting the Current,* which came out in 2005.